WAYNE STINNETT

All Ahead Full

A JESSE MCDERMITT NOVEL

Caribbean Adventure Series
Volume 22

DOWN ISLAND PRESS

Copyright © 2021
Published by DOWN ISLAND PRESS, LLC, 2021
Beaufort, SC
Copyright © 2021 by Wayne Stinnett
Library of Congress cataloging-in-publication Data
Stinnett, Wayne
All Ahead Full/Wayne Stinnett
p. cm. - (A Jesse McDermitt novel)
ISBN: 978-1-956026-03-0
Cover photograph and graphics by Aurora Publicity
Edited by Marsha Zinberg, The Write Touch
Final Proofreading by Donna Rich
Interior Design by Aurora Publicity
Down Island Press, LLC, a Down Island Publishing company.

This is a work of fiction. Names, characters, and incidents are either the
product of the author's imagination or are used fictitiously. Any
resemblance to actual persons, living or dead, businesses, companies,
events, or locales is entirely coincidental. Many real people are used
fictitiously in this work, with their permission. Most of the locations
herein are also fictional or are used fictitiously. However, the author
takes great pains to depict the location and description of the many
well-known islands, locales, beaches, reefs, bars, and restaurants
throughout the Florida Keys and the Caribbean to the best of his ability.

If you'd like to receive my newsletter, please sign up on my website.

WWW.WAYNESTINNETT.COM.

Once a month, I'll bring you insights into my private life and writing habits, with updates on what I'm working on, special deals I hear about, and new books by other authors that I'm reading.

The Jerry Snyder Caribbean Mystery Series

Wayward Sons

The Charity Styles Caribbean Thriller Series

Merciless Charity
Ruthless Charity
Reckless Charity

Enduring Charity
Vigilant Charity
Lost Charity

The Jesse McDermitt Caribbean Adventure Series

Fallen Out
Fallen Palm
Fallen Hunter
Fallen Pride
Fallen Mangrove
Fallen King
Fallen Honor
Fallen Tide
Fallen Angel
Fallen Hero
Rising Storm

Rising Fury
Rising Force
Rising Charity
Rising Water
Rising Spirit
Rising Thunder
Rising Warrior
Rising Moon
Rising Tide
Steady As She Goes
All Ahead Full
Man Overboard

The Gaspar's Revenge Ship's Store is open.

There, you can purchase all kinds of swag related to my books. You can find it at

WWW.GASPARS-REVENGE.COM

To my very good friend, Nick Sullivan, the voice behind Jesse McDermitt and all my characters. Nick was the sixty-third voice actor to audition for my first audiobook in 2015, and I'm glad I waited. He hit it out of the park with his rendition of Rusty Thurman and Jimmy Saunders. Since that day, we've become close friends, and co-host a livestream called Talk Write, where we interview other author/narrator teams. Thanks for putting a voice to all my characters. You've made my writing a lot better.

"Old friend, there are people, young and old, that I like, and people that I do not like. The former are always in short supply. I am turned off by humorless fanaticism, whether it's revolutionary mumbo-jumbo by a young one, or loud lessons from scripture by an old one. We are all comical, touching, slapstick animals, walking on our hind legs, trying to make it a noble journey from womb to tomb, and the people who can't see it all that way bore hell out of me."

— Travis McGee, *Dress Her in Indigo*

MAPS

Jesse's island in the Content Keys

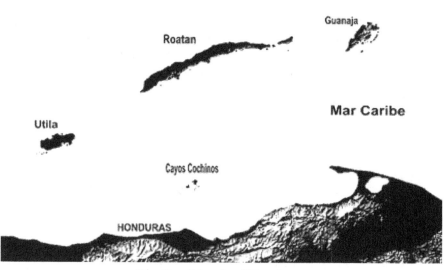

The Bay Islands of Honduras

CHAPTER ONE

The plaintive chuffing of a jaguar could be heard somewhere deep in the dense jungle. Its short, throaty, almost barking sound only carried for a short distance, whereas the great cat's roar resounded loudly for miles.

To most, the roar was a terrifying noise, especially at night. Few knew of the chuffing sound the big cats made while preoccupied. But it was a sound that Aldrick knew well.

The Río Plátano was the ancestral home of many indigenous, primitive tribes, going back to the beginning, when early man first arrived in the Americas. Aldrick had been born not far from where he now hid, crouched among the giant roots of a ceiba tree, waiting for activity on the trail. He'd felt safe in the jungle at an early age, away from his parents and the nomadic troupe they called home. Even as a little boy, he'd somehow sensed it was the place his people ought to be, not penned up in boxes called houses. He'd reconnected with his ancestral home thirty years after leaving, and had instantly felt the pull of his roots.

The jaguar, feared by nearly every animal in the jungle, was king. On a trip into the Amazon, Aldrick had once seen a female jaguar leap into the river from a high ledge and come up with a large black caiman in its powerful jaws. The jaguar was the third largest cat in the world and the second most dangerous predator in the Honduran jungle. The people Aldrick was waiting for in near total darkness were at the top of that list.

Lately, Aldrick had seen more and more drug activity in the reserve. The trail he was watching was a secret to most, but he'd learned of its existence shortly after the men had hacked their way to the interior.

Aldrick knew about their other trails as well.

The chuffing of the lone jaguar was close, but Aldrick felt no fear. He could already hear the *narcotraficantes* coming down the trail. They were in a lot more danger than he was.

They were moving and making noise.

Just to be sure, Aldrick reached into the side pocket of his vest and withdrew a small box. He opened it and drew out a fragile glass tube, then put the box away and tossed the vial lightly onto the trail, where the glass broke soundlessly. Then he sat back and waited.

Aldrick had discovered the trail two days earlier and had set up a blind on a slight rise, tucked among the buttress roots of a ceiba tree.

The massive roots, some half a meter thick and often standing two meters in height, spread out across the ground in serpentine wall patterns, supporting the tree's great weight.

The date and time of movement along the trail had been recorded in a small notebook, along with Aldrick's observations of what the men carried and an estimate of weight. Though he was Tawahka, one of the many indigenous tribes of Honduras, he was a well-educated man.

Spending many days in one place was nothing new for Aldrick. He'd spent eight days in one spot before, just watching the goings-on in his beloved rainforest. He knew the flowers, the trees, the insects, animals, and birds. He knew the sounds of the forest and how they changed from day to night. He was at home there.

Aldrick was moving toward the late years of life, growing older and wiser with the years. He'd attended university as a young man; his natural curiosity and intellect giving him an edge over the other students, even though he was perceived by some as being from a backward, primitive culture.

After receiving double degrees in biological science and environmental studies, he'd worked tirelessly, pushing for laws to protect the ecosystem, demanding to be heard. But because of his heritage, his protestations over logging and poaching went largely ignored.

So, he'd returned to the ivied halls, studying, learning all that he could while earning multiple doctoral degrees.

While the world paid little heed to an educated young man, as a tenured professor of biology in his middle years, they'd listened. Laws were passed protecting the forest and all its inhabitants. But there were always those who simply ignored the laws. Or worse.

Over the last several years, many of his peers—environmental activists and scholars—had been murdered. The killings served to shut the collective mouths of the conservation community in Honduras. The situation was akin to a sealed cesspool, the pressure of bio-decay building until it was about to explode.

Money and greed were winning, but up until the killings had started, activists like Aldrick were beginning to make inroads, finding favor with certain newly-elected government officials. The situation was starting to change.

Education among his people had mostly been parent-to-child. The young of the troupe were taught to survive and the whole tribe took part, teaching and learning from one another. Children learned to fish the rivers and hunt small game in the forest. They were taught what berries and nuts to gather and which ones to avoid. But even with no formal education, his people knew that this world was their home. Those in the cities, with all their education, technology, and toys, treated Earth as if they had somewhere else to go. The pacified indigenous tribes in the villages weren't much different. It was at one such village that he'd learned of a long lost brother, now locked in a struggle against extinction.

The drug cartels had clear-cut large parts of the primordial forest to make room for the coca plants. The coca grew well in the rich, dark soil and men became wealthy. They soon found that some of the trees they'd been slashing and burning were actually quite valuable in their own right.

Everything in their world revolved around money.

So, the cartels went into the lumber business, finding that harvesting the trees of the forest was nearly as profitable as making cocaine. The mahogany, cocobolo, rosewood, and ziricote trees were highly prized. The fact that they were endangered and protected didn't matter to the drug barons. The animals of the forest were likewise captured or killed, then sold on the black market.

When the voices of environmentalists became too loud, the drug cartels had upped the ante, sending men to hunt down and kill the people involved in protecting the natural resources. They preyed on innocent people, like a jaguar would stalk the agouti or tapir.

Various predators lived in the rainforests. Each relied on different skills and senses to find their prey. The harpy eagle, one of the most common large raptors in Honduras, relied almost exclusively on their keen eyesight. The jungle was also home to many species of owls, which also relied on sharp vision, especially at night, but they also had excellent hearing. Bats depended almost entirely on their hearing ability. Turkey vultures could track their injured prey for miles just from the smell.

But the jaguar used all its senses to find its food. Keen eyesight, even at night, coupled with exceptional hearing and sense of smell, put the jaguar at the very top of the food chain. As dangerous as men can be, most cowered in fear at the sound of an adult jaguar roaring in the night.

Even the great cat's sense of touch was tuned to the vibrations it felt through the ground or tree branch on which it stood, giving it an edge over its prey. And few animals weren't on the jaguar's menu.

Aldrick heard the soft sound of a rotten twig snap. He froze, holding his breath in mid-exhale. The sound was close, just a few meters off to his left. Out of the corner of his eye he saw a black apparition move slowly past his hiding spot. He heard the chuffing sound again, very faint, then a low growl, which was barely discernable over the sound of the men twenty meters away. Aldrick didn't flinch or turn. To do so would mean a grisly death.

Finally, the jaguar, an almost completely black female he'd observed many times, moved into the view of the night-vision goggles he wore under his hat. She paused, crouched low, and Aldrick could see her nose twitching as she homed in on the scent he'd thrown.

The great cat moved closer, its shoulders rolling with each step, totally focused on the approaching men.

The lead *narcotraficante* passed the spot where the glass vial had landed. Aldrick counted four men, each carrying a small pack on his back. He estimated the packs contained about ten to fifteen kilos, based solely on how the men moved. The first of the four was armed with a rifle. He reached a bend in the trail and disappeared, the light from his flashlight appearing and disappearing as he moved away through the thick jungle.

The jaguar began moving faster. Aldrick had watched them attack other animals; stalking slowly until they were close enough, then moving faster and faster, as fewer obstacles separated them from their quarry. The last ten or fifteen meters were a sprint, as they stretched their bodies to gobble up the distance.

The last man in the line didn't even hear her until the jaguar made its final soundless leap, tackling him from behind, its fangs sinking deep into the neck and shoulder as its hind talons tore into the man's pack, clothing, and flesh. The animal didn't snarl or growl. It was simply working—killing its prey as swiftly as possible.

A primal scream split the air as blood and white powder flew everywhere. The next man in line simply dropped his pack and ran headlong into the man in front of him.

The jaguar's victim died or passed out in mid-scream. The great cat didn't need to release or adjust her bite, but simply lifted her head high, holding her prey by the collarbone, and dragging the limp body between her legs into the night. She didn't care whether the man was dead or unconscious. He would be a meal for her and the two cubs Aldrick knew she had in her den, just two kilometers upstream.

It was over before the man with the rifle could even turn around, and by the time he got back to the bend in the trail, the jaguar and her dinner were nowhere to be seen.

Aldrick had watched the event unfold in just a matter of seconds, aided by the night-vision goggles. They allowed him to see clearly and be able to write in his ledger. He scanned the jungle and trail. The only thing left was the white powder scattered everywhere, blood dripping from a few leaves, and the man's hat, lying in the middle of the trail where he'd died.

CHAPTER Two

December 6, 2021
Utilla, Bay Islands of Honduras

The sun felt warm on my skin, as did the sand. Not hot by any stretch. After all, it was winter. But temperatures in the tropics at this time of year rarely rose above eighty-five degrees, and that wouldn't be until later in the day.

The breeze was refreshing to the skin as it came across Blackish Point. Beyond the point was Rock Harbor, where it picked up a little chill from the water, which was a few degrees cooler than the air.

The wind carried the typical scent of the tropics—fragrant flowers, salt, and decaying seaweed. There were other scents on the breeze—exotic smells, barely discernable or unidentifiable. Those fragrances were carried, scattered, and intermingled with others across thousands of miles of ocean.

I lay on my back on the warm sand, feet pointed toward the water, letting the sun and wind dry my skin. The sun had risen a couple of hours earlier and the sky was a deep cerulean with no trace of clouds or moisture. Though I had my dive watch on, I wasn't interested in the time. I was relaxed beyond belief, not a worry in the world.

Hearing a splash, I raised myself up onto my elbows, looking out toward the water. Savannah had her mask perched on her head, carrying her fins in her left hand. She lifted her knees high, like a majorette in a homecoming parade. It was the unhurried walk of a woman who was in the moment, comfortable in her own skin. It made for quite a sexy exhibition.

She wore a blue bikini, cut high over wide hips. Her long, blond hair was dark and wet, hanging down over her shoulders, and dripping rivulets of water over her tanned, flat belly. She moved with the grace and ease of a world-class athlete.

I smiled as she came up the beach toward me, her hips making a figure-eight motion as her feet churned through the powdery sand.

"You look comfortable," she said, laying her gear on top of mine in the dive bag. "But you're going to be covered with sand."

"I can return it to the sea with a quick dip." I said.

She dropped to her knees beside me, tucking her feet under her as she used a towel to wring the water from her hair.

"I could literally stay here forever," she said, turning her face toward the sun and arching her back.

I admired her long torso. Savannah never had to work hard to stay in shape. She ate healthily and exercised moderately, but in a swimsuit, her body was as breathtaking as the first time we'd met twenty years earlier.

I turned my head and looked out over the water. She was right. Utila was everything a tropical paradise was supposed to be. Palms swayed in the light air, the fronds rustling gently. The water near shore was turquoise but quickly gave way to indigo in the depths not far from shore. We were the only people on the white-sand beach.

ALL AHEAD FULL

Surrounded by warm, crystal-clear water, Utila was situated about halfway between the Tropic of Cancer and the equator, so the climate was always comfortable if you didn't mind an occasional warm, tropical rain.

It was the third largest of eight islands and fifty-three small cays that made up the Bay Islands of Honduras. The islands were the hilltops of an emerging ridge, surrounded by abysmal depths.

Almost completely ringed by a near-shore reef, Utila, as well as the largest island, Roatan, were a scuba diving and snorkeling wonderland, with nearly every dive site accessible from the beach.

Whether it was the coolest winter night or the warmest summer day, shorts and a T-shirt were perfectly comfortable.

"Yeah," I agreed. "A person could definitely get used to this."

"But," she said.

"I know. We have to get back to *Ambrosia*."

The former yacht, now research vessel, lay at anchor in sixty feet of water, just a quarter mile off the beach. The outflow of sediment from Turtle Harbor to the south created a relatively shallow, sandy shelf. Just a few hundred feet beyond her, the bottom dropped precipitously to two thousand feet or more. The near vertical wall, topped with a fringing reef, and surrounding the seven-mile-long island, was one of the main attractions for divers.

We'd stopped in the Bay Islands for some well-deserved rest and relaxation. The crew needed it, and I was quickly finding out that I did, as well. After a grueling two-month assignment in the Mediterranean, I was happy to be back in the Caribbean. Our next assignment was weeks away, on the Pacific side of Central America. Since most of the crew were divers, I'd decided on the Bay Islands of Honduras, particularly Utila, since I'd never been there.

"It will be lunchtime soon," Savannah reminded me. "Marcos

and Grady promised lionfish tacos."

I turned to face her. "Do you have any regrets?"

Her blue eyes met mine and she smiled. "Regrets about what?"

"Life aboard *Ambrosia*? Raising a son at our age? Being married to a notorious boat bum?"

"None," she replied. "Do you?"

I grinned. "Actually, I kinda like being a notorious boat bum."

"Is something bothering you, Jesse?"

"I wouldn't blame you for having second thoughts," I said. "This is a lot different from your life on *Sea Biscuit*."

She pointed out toward the boat. "Do you not see that? Compared to *Sea Biscuit*, *Ambrosia* is like living in both the Verdier houses, all rolled into one."

When we'd visited her hometown before the assignment in the Med, we'd walked up and down Bay Street in downtown Beaufort, and strolled through the neighborhood called The Point, where all the old mansions stood. She'd told me something about every house we'd passed. Not about friends she'd known, who'd lived in them when she was a girl, but the historical aspect of the homes. When we'd walked past a beautiful estate and she'd called it the Verdier House, I'd told her I was confused, because she'd earlier called another house on the main drag by the same name.

She'd explained that the father had built his house on Bay Street in 1804, and his son had built a house on The Point ten years later. Both were magnificent homes. Yet both were built for just a single family.

"*Ambrosia* has a lot more people," I reminded her.

"It can get small," she said. "But sitting on the foredeck at night puts everything right back into perspective."

"What about starting over as parents?"

"I'll admit, it wasn't what I'd envisioned earlier this year. But no, I love Alberto and can't imagine a life without him in it. To be honest, I felt a little lost when Flo left for college. All I'd been for nearly two decades was a mom. It's been the one constant in my life for so long. But it is kind of odd to *still* be a mom so late in life."

"Come on," I said, rolling forward and up onto my feet.

She wasn't far off the mark, and I was older than her. There were only two children aboard *Ambrosia*, Alberto and Fernando, who was the son of the assistant engineer. Trading parenting advice with a man who was younger than two of my daughters was awkward.

I grabbed the bag and slung it over one shoulder as Savannah got up from the sand. We walked down to the shallows and rinsed each other off. She only had sand on her knees and shins, but my whole back was covered. Still, I made sure to rinse her legs all the way up to her thighs.

We walked along the shallows, back to where we'd left the stand-up paddle boards. I put the gear bag on mine, just forward of center, and climbed on.

The two of us paddled lazily back out toward the boat in water that could barely muster a six-inch roller. We could see the bottom and watched as fish darted around and between us.

"Is that really all that's bothering you?" Savannah asked when we were halfway.

"Nothing ever really *bothers* me," I said. "I just don't want you ever to be unhappy."

"Well, I'm not," she said. "And you know I'd tell you if I were."

It took a little more than five minutes to reach the work platform at the stern of the boat. I'd lowered the aluminum platform until the deck was awash as soon as we'd anchored the ship and launched the tenders, to make it easier for divers to get in and out

11

of the water. We only had to step off the paddle boards onto the deck before the skeg hit the edge.

The garage was open, as it had been since shortly after we'd dropped anchor. The storage area under the cockpit contained two twenty-four-foot tenders, two personal watercraft, a dozen paddle boards and kayaks, as well as enough dive gear to put half the crew in the water at once. There were also two hookah rigs for bottom-cleaning, and air compressors for refilling tanks and providing air through hoses to the hookahs.

We carried the boards into the garage and Savannah pulled on a tank dress she'd left folded on a shelf and I threw on a dry Salt Life T-shirt.

Inside, I noticed six dive tanks being filled in the cooling tub. Compressed air is hot, so putting the tanks in a water tub kept the temperature down. Cooler air was denser, so the tanks could be filled to a higher capacity.

I checked the gauges, and they were all nearly half full. The compressor was set to shut off automatically at 3,000 psi.

"Everything okay?" Savannah asked, putting the paddles into a large barrel with several others.

"The tenders are still out," I said. "Just wondering who was filling the tanks."

We left the garage and went up the starboard steps to the cockpit above it, where we found two of the crew relaxing in the shade of the hardtop.

"How was the snorkeling, Captain?" Jocko Landris asked, his smile nearly as broad as his shoulders.

Jocko and the woman he was sitting with, Emma Hall, were both from Bimini, though Jocko was originally from Florida. He was a big man, easily over 250 pounds, but he had the calmest, most serene demeanor of any man I'd ever met.

"Just what the doctor ordered," I replied. "I thought you two went on the morning dive?"

"We did," Emma replied. "But we decided to just do one tank. The others dropped us off on the way to the next dive site."

"That explains the tanks in the water tub," Savannah said.

"I got it set to stop at three thousand," Jocko said, looking at his watch. "Then I'll monitor them and top each one up to thirty-two hundred."

"They're about half full," I said, then we continued into the mess hall.

Jocko was a deckhand, doing all the jobs that required muscle. Not that he was lacking in brains; he was smart, very articulate, and held a divemaster certification, as well as one for equipment specialist. He'd told me once that his parents were both large people, as were his brothers and sisters. The man could probably bench-press a Harley-Davidson.

Emma was a Bimini native and worked on the mess deck, which was run like a restaurant, with a full menu for breakfast, lunch, or dinner every six hours. She and another woman were both hostess and servers. With forty-one people on board, mealtime usually had twenty or so crew members rotating through the mess hall during the two-hour meal.

"So, what's the plan for the rest of the morning?" Savannah asked, as we both sat down at a table.

I looked over at her, grinning. "Oh, I can think of a couple of things to do that might be fun."

CHAPTER Three

The clicking of claws on teak announced Finn's arrival, just ahead of Alberto and Fernando.

"We saw you paddling back," Alberto said. "Did you see us waving from the window?"

I grinned at him. "Those windows are tinted so dark I doubt you could see in from right outside them."

"Can I get you something, Captain?" Emma asked, coming through the glass sliding door.

To make things easier on the galley staff, meals were served at prescribed hours—0500, 1100, 1700, and 2300, with Marcos and Grady alternating meals. It was an hour before the midday meal.

I waved her off. "Thanks, Emma. We're just soaking up the AC for a minute."

"I meant to ask earlier, will you be doing the lesson on the foredeck again this evening?"

After a skirmish in a bar on Grenada several months ago, I'd let it slip that I'd once taught self-defense, which wasn't actually true. I'd been a LINE fighting instructor for a short time in the Marine Corps.

LINE was an acronym for Linear Involuntary Neurological-overriding Engagement, the hand-to-hand combat all Marine infantrymen learned. The Corps was big on acronyms. LINE wasn't self-defense but combat fighting. It was a mix of several martial arts disciplines, including karate, tae kwon do, jujitsu, and Krav Maga, the technique used by the Israeli Army. The methods used were meant to kill or incapacitate the enemy swiftly and, in most cases, permanently.

Since then, a few of the crew had come to me and asked for instructions on how they could defend themselves better in the event of an attack. Emma and her friend, Nancy Graves, who also worked in the mess hall, were the first to ask. They'd both narrowly escaped being kidnapped by human traffickers.

So, every Monday evening since then, I'd instructed anyone who wanted to learn the fine art of extreme violence. If we were anchored, we did it on the roomy foredeck, and if we were underway, we moved the tables in the mess hall. Being amidships and on a lower deck, there was far less movement there.

"Yeah," I replied to Emma. "But why don't we go ashore after dark? We can do it on the beach."

She looked at me puzzled. "Why there?"

"The foredeck is nice and flat," I said. "And the padded sun lounge is comfortable when you take a fall. But how often do you think you might be attacked in such a place and in broad daylight?"

"I hadn't thought of that."

"Plus, there are numerous things you can find on a beach or in a street that can be used as an improvised weapon of chance."

She smiled. "I'll let the others know."

"Hello, Captain," Mayra Santiago said, as she came up the spiral staircase that climbed from the crew deck to the bridge. "How are you, Savannah?"

"I'm fine," my wife replied. "We just got back from the beach."

16

"The boys are taking a break," she said to Savannah, then turned toward me. "They are both doing so well. Alberto's handwriting skills have improved quite a bit since you suggested writing letters to your friend in Florida."

When Mayra told me that Alberto was a little behind in his writing skills, I'd suggested he write a letter every day to my friend Rusty Thurman, back home in Marathon. Not on a keyboard, but using pencil and paper. Once written, the letters were scanned and emailed to Rusty, and he'd written back to each one, in his own flourished handwriting.

"Glad to hear that, Mayra," I said. "It's a shame writing skills are no longer taught in most public schools."

"We're going to take Finn outside," Alberto said.

"Don't forget to hose down the grass," I told him.

The boys led Finn out the big, sliding-glass door, then up to the port side deck, where Jack Armstrong had gone to great expense to create a small grassy patch on the stern.

Savannah looked over at me with a sad smile.

"You miss him a lot," I said.

She nodded and quickly averted her eyes.

When we'd returned to Marathon from Beaufort last August, Woden had become very lethargic. Though he'd been almost thirteen, which was pretty old for large-breed dogs like the Rottweiler, he'd seemed perfectly healthy until then. I'd thought he was only tired from all the traveling. We took him to a vet, who told us he was dying.

Flo had come down from Gainesville the night we learned there was nothing the vet could do. Woden had been her guardian and friend since she was a little girl. Later that evening, he passed peacefully in his sleep, his big head on her lap as she gently stroked the fur between his eyes and cried.

Savannah rose and pulled on my hand. "Come on. We should go get cleaned up before lunch."

We left and went up the port steps to the side deck. The boys waved from the stern as we went forward, and I opened a hatch to an inside passageway that led from the command bridge back to my office and our private quarters.

"Have you heard anything from Jack on how the *Phoenix* is coming along?" Savannah asked, as we entered our stateroom.

"As a matter of fact, he emailed this morning and sent a picture."

I picked up my Metis tablet, opened the email from Jack and turned it to her. "They already have the hull finished and the superstructure is near so."

She took the Metis and looked at the photo. "Wow! I didn't realize the bow would be so high. It looks like an icebreaker."

"The design is sort of a modern interpretation of an old galleon, with a high fo'c'sle that will house the labs."

"And where will our cabin be?"

"Just like on a galleon," I said, opening the fridge for a couple of beers. I handed her one. "But it's hardly a cabin at nearly two thousand square feet. It's at the uppermost part of the stern, just aft the VIP quarters and bridge deck."

She put the Metis down and opened her bottle. "It doesn't look very fast—not exactly streamlined."

"Doesn't matter," I said, opening the door to our private terrace and following her out. "With a fifty-megawatt nuclear powerplant, the engineers say that wind resistance is a minor concern. They estimate she'll be capable of sustained speeds above forty knots, with a top speed of just over fifty."

"What's fifty megawatts in terms I'm familiar with?"

"A lot," I replied. "Nearly seventy thousand horsepower."

Savannah sat down in a chaise lounge, stretching her long, tan legs out. "You mentioned VIP cabins. What's that about?"

She hadn't shown much interest until lately. I guess the knowledge that we'd be moving in about a year onto a ship that could literally go anywhere without stopping was beginning to pique her curiosity.

"Some of the VIPs will be semi-permanent crew members. The fo'c'sle will be all about science—studying the ocean, the sea floor, wind patterns, storms, the effects of global warming, and such. The VIP quarters are for visiting scientists. Jack says that many of them will stay on nearly full time, like regular crew, but won't have any ship duties."

"I didn't think you believed in all those global warming predictions."

"I don't," I said, sitting beside her. "Looking back over billions of years of climate data, anyone can see that we're heading toward another ice age and that the world is much cooler today than it has been in the past."

"But you can't deny global temperatures are on the rise since the industrial age."

"People freak out because it's risen a tenth of a degree in the last hundred years, but a hundred *million* years ago, it was *seven* degrees warmer than this past century's average."

"That was about the time the first warm-blooded animals appeared," she said, sipping her beer and looking out over the water behind us.

I gave her a puzzled look. Savannah lived in the moment and always had.

"I read it somewhere," she said, looking over at me and giving a slight shrug.

"It was," I agreed. "The last ice age was two hundred million years before that, and it was only four degrees cooler than today's average."

"So, we're closer to bobsledding in Miami than sunbathing in Anchorage?"

I nodded. "Two extremes separated by only eleven degrees of warmth. Temperatures over the last hundred million years have been steadily declining. Sure, it bounces up and down, but falling overall. What's happened in the last hundred years is a change in weather, not climate change. Jack's icebreaker design may yet come in handy."

"But not in our lifetime," she said.

I laughed. "Definitely not. Probably not even in the next thousand generations. But still, if humans can alter weather patterns by accident, we should be able to correct it on purpose. It's not like we have another planet to go to."

"Where will *Phoenix* go?"

"All over the world," I replied, then took a pull from my Red Stripe. "From Antarctica to the Northern Passage, but primarily in the tropics."

"That's good," Savannah said. "You know I don't do cold very well. When the ice age comes, we're moving to Ecuador."

I'd once thought the notion that humans could change Earth's climate was preposterous and gave greater credence to human impact on this planet than deserved. But I couldn't deny recent studies. Could it be corrected? Could mankind manage the temperature of Earth so that it remained comfortable, like changing the setting on a thermostat? I doubted it. Earth had gone through numerous cycles of warming and cooling and would continue to do so. Human presence on the big blue rock was nothing more than the blink of an eye for Methuselah.

But I'm not a scientist. To think that within a year or so I'd be in command of a nuclear-powered research vessel full of them was stretching my own imagination. Let alone the fact that it would be powered by an engine I knew next to nothing about.

I heard the hatch inside open and close, then Alberto and Finn came out onto the terrace.

"Me and Fernando are going back down for our afternoon lessons," he said.

"Fernando and I," Savannah corrected him.

"Yeah," he said. "Anyway, we brought Finn back first. Can we go snorkeling after?"

"Sure," I replied. "If you want, we can break out the hookah and inspect the bottom of the boat together."

"Cool!" he exclaimed, then dashed off.

"Really?" Savannah asked. "Don't you think they're a little young?"

"Rusty's daughter, Julie, was scuba diving at seven and was certified the week she turned twelve and was old enough. Since then, the minimum age for open-water certification has been lowered to ten. Alberto can take a dive class next June. Besides, we won't be going more than ten feet."

The speaker mounted on the wall clicked and Matt Brand's voice came over it. "Cap'n McDermitt to the bridge."

"Duty calls," I said, rising from the chair and pushing the button next to the com. "On my way, Matt."

CHAPTER FOUR

The passageway from our quarters to the bridge was the length of the operations center just aft the bridge deck. My deck shoes made a squeaking sound on the painted aluminum deck as I strode forward. At the end, I stepped through the hatch and onto the bridge.

"Wasson, mate?" I asked Matt, in a terrible English accent.

Matt was from Cornwall, England, as his family had been for several centuries. The Cornish people had their own dialect, which I hadn't yet mastered. Sometimes, I didn't even understand what he was saying.

"*Myttin da*, Cap'n," he greeted me—the Cornish way of saying good morning. "There's a Honduran patrol boat a headin' this way."

Matt was dressed as usual, blue trousers and crisp white shirt, with his first mate's hat sitting rakishly atop his curly, light-brown hair. While at anchor, the two of us, along with ten other senior bridge and security people, alternated two-hour shifts on the bridge, with two people on duty at all times.

"It's from the mainland," Giselle Lopez said, bent over the chart plotter. "Not from Roatan. A SAFE Boats 35 Interceptor, manufactured in the United States."

Giselle was Fernando's mother and the oldest of Mayra and

Marcos Santiago's three daughters. We'd picked her and the rest of the family up several months ago. They'd been miles from shore, in a broken-down, leaky boat, trying to flee their native Venezuela. Since then, she'd become a valuable asset on the bridge as Yeoman Val McLarin's assistant. She soaked up information like a dry sponge.

"What's a patrol boat from the mainland want with us?" I asked nobody in particular.

I glanced at the boat's location on the chart plotter and picked up the binoculars. Utila was twenty miles from the mainland, and we were on the north side of the island.

Through the binos, I could see the patrol boat racing toward us. It was far too close to shore to be running at such a speed. Most of Utila's dive sites, like Roatan's, were accessed from shore and divers used little more than a floating dive flag to mark their location in the water.

"Bleddy numpties goin' way too fast, yeah?" Matt said.

I lowered the binos and looked over at him. "Did they hail us?"

"Oye, Cap'n. Before they was even in sight. Told us to heave to and prepare to be boarded."

"Boarded?"

"Aye."

"Anything else?"

Matt shook his head. "Nothin' since then."

I didn't want to have a run-in with the Honduran Navy. Armstrong had contacts in many places—civilian governments, law enforcement agencies, and many countries' militaries. But I also didn't want to be a sitting duck for some over-zealous officer or some smuggler who stole a boat.

The patrol boat was angling toward our port side.

I punched a button on the intercom console. "Bridge to security.

I want two men, covertly armed, in the cockpit."

"On the way," Walt Meachum, the security team's armorer, replied.

"Let's go down and meet the boat," I said to Matt, then turned to Giselle. "Hold down the fort."

"The fort?" she asked.

Though she'd gone to college in the States, Giselle was a native Venezuelan and hadn't yet picked up on a lot of American colloquialisms.

"You're in charge of the bridge," I said, as Matt and I went out the port hatch.

We met Walt and the youngest member of the security team, Duster, in the cockpit. To the north, the patrol boat began to slow and turn toward us.

"Who are they?" Walt asked, watching the thirty-five-foot patrol boat coming closer.

"Honduran Navy," Matt said. "They mean to board us."

"Your orders?" Duster asked.

Dustin Alexander, or Duster, as most called him, was also formerly enlisted in the Army. Nearly everyone in the service got a nickname, and his was just a mashup of his first and last name. I knew a guy whose last name was Alewine, and he, of course, became known as Wino. I was called Too Tall for a while. After being wounded in action, Duster had left the service and gone to medical school. He was still waiting to go into residency, but for now, he was the de facto medic aboard *Ambrosia*.

"I just want you guys to be ready," I said. "The boat's from the mainland and radioed for us to heave to and wait to be boarded."

"Heave to?" Walt asked. "We've been anchored here for almost two days."

"Just one of the things that makes this a little hinky," I said. "Just be on your toes and follow my lead."

I led the way down the port steps to the large aluminum work platform built onto *Ambrosia's* stern.

"Raise the platform to dock level," I said to Matt.

I waited on one of the lower steps as Matt went to the controls and activated the hydraulics. As he raised the platform, water poured off and sloshed back on, as the ship rode up and down in the small rollers. He continued bringing it up until the whole thing was two feet above the water. Then we all walked out to the edge.

Two men stood in the front of the boat, both armed with American-made M-4 rifles. One had a coil of dock line in his hand, ready to throw, while the other stood with his rifle slung on his chest at the ready.

As the boat turned broadside, I could see two more men at the covered helm area. One of them stepped out to the gunwale and removed his dark sunglasses.

He looked straight at Matt. "Are you the captain?" he barked in barely accented English.

"I'm the captain," I said. "Jesse McDermitt."

It was a natural mistake, and I didn't fault the guy—Matt was in uniform, and I was still in my board shorts and T-shirt. But it threw the man off slightly.

He looked from Matt to me. "I am *Alferez de Fragata* Jorge Flores," the man said. "My man will throw a line."

"Frigate ensign," Matt said out of the side of his mouth. "A regular ensign in yer Navy."

I glanced over at him, and he shrugged. "Issa hobb, mind."

I nodded at Duster, who stepped forward and caught the line, then quickly made it fast to a recessed deck cleat.

"Have him throw another from the stern and we'll bring you alongside."

Ensign Flores gave the men in the bow an order in Spanish, and they moved quickly aft and threw another line.

"May I ask the purpose of this visit?" I asked the officer.

"We are going to board your vessel and search for contraband."

"Contraband?" I asked. "Do you mean like illegal drugs?"

"No, *Capitán*. Illegal animals."

"There's only one animal aboard *Ambrosia*," I said. "My yellow Lab, Finn."

"Then you will have no problem with my having a look," Flores said, as he stepped over onto the platform.

I glared at him. "I cannot stop you," I said. "You can board any vessel in Honduran waters at any time. But it's always courteous to ask first."

"I am not a courteous man," Flores said. "And we do not live in polite times."

"Very well," I said, waving a hand toward the garage behind us. "This is our storage area; feel free to start there."

He nodded to the two men who'd thrown the lines and they disappeared into the garage.

Flores looked over at the bright yellow submersible resting in its cradle on the starboard side. "A most unusual toy for a yacht owner."

"*Ambrosia* is a research vessel," I said. "We are not a pleasure craft."

This seemed to surprise him, then one of his men called from inside, and the surprised look evaporated.

He waved a hand toward the garage. "If you please, *Capitán*."

"*Nada aquí,*" one of the men said, as we entered, "*excepto una puerta cerrada.*"

"Why is this door locked?" Flores turned and asked me.

"It's not a door," I said, moving to the intercom. "It's a watertight hatch to the engine room. It's always closed and dogged from the inside."

I pushed the engine room button on the console. "Captain to engineering."

"Yes, *Capitán?*" Ricardo Lopez, the assistant engineer asked.

"Open the hatch to the garage, Ricardo."

A moment later, there was a metallic click and the dogs retracted. Ricardo pushed the hatch open and looked out.

"After you, Ensign," I said, extending a hand toward the opening. "This is my assistant engineer, Ricardo Lopez."

I followed him through, and his two men trailed me. Duster and Walt came right behind them, with Matt bringing up the rear.

"*Madre Dios,*" Flores muttered, staring down at the twin Paxman V-18 diesels and a pair of Lycoming ETF40B auxiliary gas turbines. The deck, bulkheads, and nearly everything else was painted a glistening white, except for the four large fuel tanks at the far end, which were yellow.

"If you wouldn't mind," I said, "please tell your men to be very careful. There's over thirty thousand gallons of fuel down here."

He looked at me a moment, then nodded at his two men, who both removed their hands from their rifles.

"What is the power?" Flores asked.

"The diesel main engines are fifty-three-hundred horsepower each, and the gas turbines are both a little more than that, but spin at a much higher rate. Just about twenty-two thousand horsepower total."

"Why do you need such power, *Capitán?*"

"We rarely do," I replied honestly, leading the way down the steps to the deck. "We operate primarily on the main engines with a cruising speed of under twenty knots. But if we need to outrun a storm, or get somewhere in a hurry, we can fire up the turbines. Each engine has its own jet drive."

Flores's two men waited on the landing.

"And you say this is a research vessel?"

I turned to face the man and lowered my voice so the others couldn't hear. "Do your superiors know that you have boarded my vessel?" I asked.

"Why do you ask?"

"Because I'm betting they don't. Would you please contact your fleet commander and give him the name of my ship and its owner, Armstrong Research?"

"There have been numerous yachts in our waters, smuggling exotic animals out of the country. I am authorized to inspect any boat I find."

"I understand that," I said, still trying to be diplomatic. "But if your commanding officer knew you were on *this* boat, he would probably tell you to move on. He might even reprimand you for boarding us."

He stared into my eyes for a moment. I didn't turn away.

"There's no contraband of any kind aboard my vessel," I said softly, then decided to risk it. "In fact, the problem you're experiencing is one of the things we try to help fix."

"Fix?" he scoffed.

"I don't want you wasting your time or getting into trouble with your superiors, Ensign Flores. Not everyone who fights greed and corruption is military or police."

When he pulled a satellite telephone from his pocket, I pointed toward the hatch. "You won't get reception down here."

He went up the steps quickly, ordering us and his men to wait.

"What is going on, *Capitán?*" Ricardo asked.

"Honduran patrol boat from the mainland," I replied. "Looking for contraband animals."

"Ah yes," Ricardo said, knowingly. "There is a growing problem in all of Latin America with poachers and smugglers. I read where over a hundred environmentalists have been murdered in Honduras in the last few years."

"Environmentalists?"

"*Si, Capitán,*" he replied. "The drug cartels are behind it, I am sure. They have been clear-cutting small, remote areas of the rainforest to grow the coca. The endangered hardwood trees they cut down are smuggled out, along with many wild animals."

"Like parrots and such?"

Ricardo nodded. "Birds, yes. But many other animals, as well. Many kinds of snakes and reptiles have been nearly wiped out; even the jaguar is becoming scarce."

"Who in bleddy hell would want a 200-pound pet cat with claws as long as me fingers?" Matt asked.

"Not all the animals are smuggled out alive," Ricardo replied.

Flores came quickly back down to the landing. He ordered his men to return to the boat, then came down to the engine room deck and faced me.

"My apologies, *Capitán.* You are free to continue on your way."

"We've been anchored here two days," I said. "We're planning to stay a while longer."

He eyed me warily. "Are you here about the poaching? My commander said this ship was a great help to local people and governments wherever it went."

I nodded toward my assistant engineer. "Ricardo was just telling me about the problems going on here. I wasn't personally aware, but I wouldn't be surprised if it wasn't something already on Armstrong's radar. But we are only here for rest and relaxation."

The disappointment in his eyes was noticeable. "I see."

I told Walt and Duster they could go on about their duties and then escorted Flores up to the garage and out into the glaring sunlight.

He stopped at the garage door, out of earshot of his men, and turned to face me. "What is Armstrong Research?"

"Oceanographic research is a cover," I said. "We have some of the best covert operatives from all over the world working with local governments and police to make the world a better place."

"I see," Flores said. "Does—"

He ended his thought mid-sentence and started to turn, but then stopped. When he looked into my eyes again, I saw pain—the all-too- familiar pain of loss.

"My sister was a conservationist," he said, his voice no longer sharp and cutting. "But that doesn't truly say it all. She was young and idealistic—an outspoken environmental activist."

"Was?"

"She was butchered last year in the streets of La Ceiba."

CHAPTER FIVE

Twenty minutes later, I walked with Ensign Jorge Flores down to his waiting boat. Neither of us said anything until they cast off.

"*Vaya con Dios,*" Jorge said, lifting a hand.

"*Estar seguro, mi amigo,*" I replied, wishing him well.

"Mind a word, Cap'n?" Matt asked, as we watched the boat move away.

"What's that?"

"Ye was with that pillock in yer office a while, yeah? Mind if I ask what ye was discussin'?"

"Gathering intel," I replied. "I'm undecided on how to proceed at the moment, though. Any of the tech guys free?"

"Ed Barkley and 'is son went back to 'the OBX,' whatever that is. I 'ear they're on the lash till after the first of the year."

"The lash?" I asked.

"You know," Matt said. "A pub crawl...er...a bender, yeah?"

"Ah, well their last assignment was a long one. They're from the Outer Banks of North Carolina—OBX."

"Anyway, Mr. Tanaka 'as some free time."

"Ask him to meet me in my office in thirty minutes," I said.

"Aye, Cap'n."

I went back to my quarters to get dressed. It was almost

lunchtime.

"That was quick," Savannah said, as I entered. "I saw the patrol boat pull up and heard you talking to them. I assumed you'd be wrapped up for a while."

"The ensign had a change in plans," I said. "I have to meet with Roger Tanaka in half an hour."

"To learn more about what you and the Honduran officer were talking about for so long?"

"His sister was murdered in La Ceiba," I said. "She was an outspoken environmentalist who was hacked to death by two men with machetes. It happened in broad daylight, right out in the street."

"And he came to *Ambrosia* seeking justice or to enlist help to get vengeance?"

I stopped at the door to our bedroom. Could Flores have already known about Armstrong? I didn't believe so. He seemed genuinely surprised. But there was still that possibility. A chance that I was being played.

"I don't think that was it," I said. "He had no idea what *Ambrosia* is or what Armstrong Research does. He said he received an anonymous tip about us and was trying to score points with his superiors."

"I'm sure Roger can find out anything that's amiss," Savannah said, following me into our bedroom.

I pulled my T-shirt over my head and stepped out of my swimsuit. "I'll just be a minute," I said, noting that she still hadn't changed, either.

Two minutes after stepping into the shower, the door to the small head opened and Savannah joined me under the powerful jets. It was a bigger shower stall than either of us had on our own boats, but not by much. Lack of room had never stopped us before and showering together was just Savannah's way of conserving water.

Once I was dressed, I went forward to my office, leaving the hatch open. I sat down at my desk and opened the laptop, which was connected to the ship's Multi-Encrypted Technical Interface System, or METIS.

I easily found several news stories about the murder. La Ceiba is a tourist city—the gateway to the Bay Islands. The killing was witnessed by several people, none of whom could give a description of the two assailants, except they were dressed in black and wore hoods.

A knock on the bulkhead interrupted me. "You wanted to see me, Captain?"

"Come in, Roger," I said. "Have a seat."

Roger Tanaka was a fourth-generation American from California. He'd told me once that his grandparents had met as teenagers in an internment camp in the early 1940s. After the Japanese bombing of Pearl Harbor, more than 100,000 people of Japanese descent, mostly along the Pacific coast, had been forcibly moved to camps in the interior of the country. Most were American citizens.

He sat on the couch, and I turned to face him. "With the Barkleys on hiatus for a few weeks, you've got some free time?"

"Yes, sir," he replied. "Is there something you need me to do?"

"There is," I said, and turned the computer screen toward him.

He looked at the image on the newspaper story—a blood-soaked white sheet covering a body, the lower half of a woman's bloody left leg sticking out. He leaned closer, reading the story, which was in Spanish. Tanaka was also fluent in French and, of course, Japanese.

"A murder in La Ceiba earlier this year?"

35

"One of many murders of environmentalists in Honduras," I said. "Her name was Luna Flores. I don't know if you saw the Honduran Navy patrol boat that visited us earlier, but the ensign in charge of it was her brother."

"No, I didn't see it," Roger said. "Did he come seeking help?"

It was rare, but Jack had told me that people in law enforcement occasionally asked the organization for assistance outside of the usual bureaucratic channels.

"Actually, he'd never heard of Armstrong," I replied. "And to be honest, I'm not sure if there's anything we can do, or even if Jack might already have someone working on it."

"I'll start there," he said. "See if any assets are working it, or if the murders are even in the system."

"Ensign Flores wanted to search the ship for illegal animals being smuggled out of the country," I explained. "These killings seem to revolve around that and the illegal cutting and clearing of the rainforest to grow coca. So, dig into that, too. I'd be real interested in knowing who the tipster was. But just on your spare time for right now. We're off duty, and I want everyone relaxed and fresh next week."

"I'm not a diver, Captain, so I have lots of free time."

"What did you do back home to unwind?" I asked, just making idle conversation.

He shrugged. "Like most California kids, I went surfing or sailing."

"Is that right?" I asked, rhetorically. "I've done a little sailing and surfing, too."

"I thought you were from the Florida Keys, sir."

In Florida, to find any good surfing spots, you'd have to head north of Miami. Surfing was almost non-existent where I grew up

36

and perhaps more so in the Keys.

"I am," I replied. "But whenever a tropical storm or hurricane blows up through the Florida Straits or into the Gulf of Mexico, we get a little surf action."

He grinned. "Like in Jimmy Buffett's *Surfing in a Hurricane?*"

"Pretty much," I said. "I'm not a good wave rider and getting pounded by those twenty-footers y'all get on the West Coast isn't real appealing at my age."

He grinned. "My uncle taught me. Long, slow breaks on a board that weighed more than me." Then he looked up at me quickly. "Anything else?"

"Get a list of all the victims—these environmentalists—and see if there's any other possible connection between them."

"Right away," Roger said.

"Thanks. That's all."

He left and I turned back to the computer. I scrolled down to the photo of a still-living Luna Flores. She was an attractive young woman—the story said she was twenty-four—with shoulder-length dark hair and light brown eyes. The picture had obviously been cropped. I could see a man's arm extending behind her shoulder at a downward angle. Somebody taller than her. Behind them were large leaves and flowers, slightly out of focus. She was smiling. She looked happy and safe.

No, not happy, I thought, looking closer. Her expression was more than that. Proud? Overjoyed?

I downloaded the image and sent it to my Armstrong satellite phone, then checked my watch. It was just after 1100 and the mess hall would be open now. I closed the laptop and went aft to our quarters.

Savannah and Alberto were just coming out. "I was about to

come get you," she said. "The last of the divers got back ten minutes ago. They had more than thirty lionfish."

Lionfish were an invasive species throughout the Caribbean. Their elaborate fins and stripes serve as a warning to most predators. The fins were venomous and could cause severe injuries.

It's believed that certain smaller predatory fish species in the Indo-Pacific region are immune to the venom and naturally keep the lionfish numbers in check by preying on the larvae and juveniles. Since those predators don't exist in the Atlantic and Caribbean, the lionfish population has flourished, so most dive operations in the Caribbean have weekly culls, where divers are encouraged to spear as many as they can.

I thumped my chest and grunted at Alberto.

He thumped his and grunted in return, "Man eating lion."

"Oh, dear Lord," Savannah said, opening the exterior hatch and turning aft. "You're turning him into a knuckle-dragger, too."

Alberto grunted again, "Ugh, ugh, hugh?"

I ruffled his mop of dark hair. "Sometimes the world needs knuckle- draggers."

We followed Savannah down the steps to the cockpit, where six tables had been arranged with four chairs at each, as well as the regular seating inside. The mess hall was set up cafeteria style, and we got in line behind Axel Troutman and Kassandra Santiago. I could smell the grilled lionfish tacos.

"Was that a Honduran patrol boat leaving just before we got back?" Axel asked.

"Yeah," I replied. "He received an anonymous tip that we were smuggling animals."

Ahead of them, Jocko Landris turned his broad shoulders and grinned back at us, putting another taco on a plate already piled high. "Only animals being smuggled here are these lionfish."

We moved through the line quickly, adding grated cheese, lettuce, tomatoes, onions, and guacamole, then moved out to the cockpit to eat. Axel and Kassandra had joined her sister, Crystal, and another member of the bridge crew, Ross Mosely. Axel was one of the ship's helmsmen and Ross was the senior navigator and sonar man.

"Why would someone say we were smuggling animals?" Axel asked, picking a piece of fish out and tasting it. "Mmm, this is good!"

"What animals?" Ross asked.

So, I went on to explain to them about Ensign Flores's visit and how his sister had been killed. Not in full, graphic detail with Alberto right there, but just that she'd been killed. I then told them what I'd learned so far, that hundreds of other conservationists had also been killed in the last couple of years.

"Roger Tanaka is looking into everything," I said. "To see what other connections the victims might have or if there's some way we can assist."

"Perfect guy for the job," Ross said. "He's big into conservation."

The idea that someone pointed at us and said "smuggler" irritated me. Could it have just been some diver who was envious of the big, fancy yacht? Or something more nefarious, like the real smuggler trying to throw off the authorities? As far as I knew, this was *Ambrosia's* first time in these waters. But she had a way of being in places where strange things happened to those who lived outside the law. Had someone on the bad side figured out Jack Armstrong's life mission?

I munched on a taco, trading glances with Savannah. Alberto's head was down, feeding. He had good table manners, but when he was eating something he really liked, he was a shoveler.

Axel was right; the fish was flaky and seared to perfection with an intoxicating blend of island spices. My friend Rufus, Rusty's Jamaican chef back at the Rusty Anchor, cooked in a similar way, blending a lot of island spices that complemented each other.

I peeked at Savannah. She was watching me eat.

"What is it?" she asked, sensing my unease.

"Someone called me a smuggler."

"I'm sure it wasn't directed toward you, personally, Jesse."

"Makes no difference," I said.

Alberto looked up from his feast and wiped the grease from his chin. "Smugglers are criminals, Dad. You're not a criminal."

I smiled at him and nodded. Yet, it still raised the short hairs on the back of my neck.

I was no choir boy; I'd done a lot of things I wasn't proud of. I'd once been adrift for over a year, nowhere to go and in a big hurry to get there. I'd become involved in things I knew I shouldn't have and with people I knew better than to associate with. I got drunk and threw my weight around, picking fights and picking up young women. I even smuggled some things. But that was a long time ago—before I got involved with Jack Armstrong.

"Well, if Roger can't get to the bottom of it," Savannah said, wiping the corner of her mouth with a napkin, "you can always call Chyrel."

"I'd rather not," I said.

Chyrel's husband, the man who'd mentored me as a Marine NCO, had just died in August after fighting cancer for nearly two years. Not fighting it with intravenous drug cocktails and radiation—by the time he'd found out, it'd already spread and was considered terminal—but fighting it by living each day he had left to the fullest. It was hard for me to accept that he was gone, especially in light of the fact he'd been in such great physical condition just a year before, rappelling out of a helicopter with me to rescue two kidnapped women in the Everglades. I didn't want to burden Chyrel when she should be grieving his loss.

"I spoke to her yesterday," Savannah said, then slipped a tiny bit of fish into her mouth and discreetly licked her fingers.

"What did y'all talk about?" I asked.

"She has two girls staying with her," she replied. "They're enrolled at the Lodge. She was just telling me about them."

"Sounds like she's staying busy."

"Not as busy as she wants to be, Jesse. She wants to work."

"She's committed to the Lodge," I said. "But I guess she can work from anywhere."

"Give her something to do," Savannah said, leaning closer toward me. "Something real. Something where she can make a difference."

CHAPTER SIX

After lunch, I put the hookah rig in the water with three low-pressure hoses attached to the big float, each connected to a first stage manifold. A high-pressure supply hose connected the first stage to *Ambrosia's* air compressor, much like it would be connected to a tank.

Most true hookah rigs had a gas engine or electric motor driving an air compressor on a big float. The compressor pressurized a single air tank with low-pressure hoses going to one or more divers under the water. It could be dragged around by the diver, providing air until the gas ran out or the battery drained.

We had two of those aboard, but the one used for inspecting and cleaning the bottom was just a float and air tank. The high-pressure air came directly from the ship's compressor. With a keel depth of only eight-and-a-half feet, a diver could stay down for quite a while, though we limited it to two hours, changing out with someone else if need be.

The boys were excited. They'd both done some snorkeling, and breathing off a hookah rig was basically the same when working at shallow depths.

I'd been teaching them the basics of scuba, and Mayra had been including a lot of dive profile calculations in their math lessons. She told me how eager both boys were to master those, using what they were learning to solve real-world math problems about the physics involved in breathing compressed air at depth.

I knew there wouldn't be a problem, since their hoses were only fifteen feet long and, without weight, they'd spend almost all their time within a few feet of the surface. Until they learned to control their breathing.

No-weight, hookah diving was a great way for someone new to diving to learn how they can control their buoyancy just with their lungs. You could see when the realization hit each one. It was almost always the same. Their body would suddenly stop moving as they tested the new skill. They'd rise a few inches exhale bubbles and drop back down.

"What will we see?" Fernando asked, looking down into the clear water.

"The underside of the boat mostly," I replied, as I clipped the high- pressure line to the rail with two hundred feet of play. That would allow the float to reach the bow. "There will probably be a few small fish under her. They like to eat the little bugs that grow on the hull."

"That's all?"

"This is work, son. But remember what I told you about work?"

"Work can be fun," he replied. "But what's so great about just seeing the boat?"

I grinned at him. "Oh, you haven't seen the boat yet. All you've seen is what's built on top of her."

"Huh?"

"Everything above the waterline isn't the boat. What makes something a boat is what's under the water. You could build all the rest on dry land, and it'd just be a weird-looking house."

"I don't get it," he replied, looking at the harnesses and hoses.

"You'll see," I told him. "Now, let's get these belts on you."

They were nothing more than weight belts with a clip for the low- pressure hose. I didn't put any weights on the boys' belts and they both would wear full-face masks. I preferred a regular mask and regulator, so I could more easily talk on the surface.

Once we all had our gear on, I reminded them about being aware of their hoses, so they didn't get tangled. We sat on the work deck, slipped our fins on, then I entered first.

When I turned and looked up at the boys, I saw Savannah, Mayra, and Giselle watching anxiously. I put my fist on top of my head, signaling Savannah that everything was alright. She returned my OK sign with anxious fingers. Both boys turned and waved.

"Okay," I said, after taking my regulator out. "Keep the loose end of your hose in your left hand and slide up to the edge of the deck. Once you're in the water, remember to move straight out away from the boat so you don't bang your head."

I could hear the short hiss of air as the valves on the regulators' second stages, which were attached to their masks, opened and closed.

"Okay," I said, as the boys sat on the edge. "Let's hookah!"

They both slid into the water, and I replaced my second stage, exhaling most of my air to sink below the surface.

The boys looked like some sort of weird water bugs, arms and legs spread wide and flailing. After a couple seconds, they got control of their fins and floated with their backs at the surface, finning away from the boat before turning to face me.

I hung vertically upright in the water just a few feet below the surface, maintaining neutral buoyancy with my breathing. My legs were crossed at the ankles, and I held my hands clasped in front, exhibiting calm.

The boys looked at me, then both tried to emulate my relaxed posture. I nodded my approval and turned toward *Ambrosia*.

The small waves on the surface moved along her hull, but she lay in the water as if she were solidly attached to the bottom, which she was, by way of three hundred feet of rode and a heavy anchor. I could just make out the chain hanging from the bow and disappearing toward the bottom, fifty-five feet below. The vis was over two hundred feet.

Before us, *Ambrosia's* hull was clean, save for fine hairs of algae growing near the surface. From beneath, the shape of the hull was revealed to us. Different hull shapes were designed with different jobs in mind. *Ambrosia's* stepped hull and deep vee design screamed speed, even when riding at anchor.

I looked back at the boys. Behind their masks, their eyes were wide in awe. They could finally *see* the boat.

CHAPTER SEVEN

That evening, just before sunset, nine of us boarded one of the twenty-four-foot tenders and headed toward the beach. After only a couple of minutes, Axel slowed to an idle and raised the outboard slightly, until the hull nudged the sandy bottom.

Ross immediately jumped onto the sand from the bow, then grabbed the anchor and carried it up the beach, jamming it into the sand.

We all climbed out and I had everyone line up at the midway point between the water and vegetation along the top of the dune.

"Up to now," I began, "we've only talked about and practiced the basics of surviving an altercation. Most of that is based on karate. What's that mean?"

"Empty hand," Emma Hall replied.

"Exactly," I said. "But what if your assailant's hands aren't empty? Axel, step up here for a minute."

He was slightly hesitant. I'd never picked just one of them, always two, using them to describe blocks and strikes against each other.

I had him stand beside me. "Now, Axel and I are about the same height and weight. But my slight edge in size is offset by his being not much more than half my age."

"Wait...what?" Axel said, looking at me. "How old are you, Captain?"

"On the day of the next equinox, I'll be sixty."

"Come on," Ross said. "You can't be much over forty."

"Well, I appreciate that," I said. "But it's true. I'm making my sixtieth trip around the sun this year. Now, based on just that information alone, would anyone think we were *not* evenly matched?"

Most nodded and a few said yeah or grunted an uh-huh.

I turned, reached into the tender, and pulled out the boat hook, a long, wooden pole with a metal tip and small hook for fending a boat away from a dock or grabbing a cleat.

Turning back, I spun it in my hands from one side of my body to the other. Then I stopped and planted the wooden end in the sand, holding the other end near the hook like I was leaning on a lamp post.

"How about now?"

Everyone laughed, including Axel, though his chuckle was somewhat nervous. I grinned at him, then tossed the hook, which he caught easily.

"And now?" I asked. "Notice how easily the balance of power can shift? Being able to defend yourself against an attacker with just your bare hands is great. But it becomes a lot easier, and often unnecessary, when you have something in your hand."

Crystal raised a small hand. I could only guess that she was there to learn something new, since, from what her father had told me, she was quite capable of defending herself. She was supposed to be an expert in Venezuelan stick fighting. Or maybe Axel talked her into it.

"You handle that hook like you've practiced with it, Captain."

48

"With this particular boat hook?" I asked, taking it back from
Axel. "No, but I've trained with a lot of similar weapons of
opportunity. The spinning isn't just for show. You get a sense of the
balance of an improvised weapon when you handle it."

I stepped forward, pulling the boat hook up like it was a
bayonetted M-16, and executed a horizontal butt stroke against an
imaginary opponent, following through with a vertical slash then a
jab.

"Almost any object can be used as a weapon of opportunity," I
said.

"How would you defend against someone who had something
like a boat hook?" Nancy Graves asked.

Nancy was the newest member of the crew, aside from the
Santiago family. She and Emma had been abducted several months
earlier, and Jocko beaten unconscious, when we were in Grenada,
and it was because of that experience that we were all on the beach.

I tossed the hook back to Axel and returned to the boat,
picking up the first thing I could find—an inflated, two-foot-long
rubber fender. It had heavy rubber loops at either end to tie a rope
to, only one of which had a short length of dock line attached with
a bowline knot.

"While it might not be the ideal weapon," I said, turning back
to the group, "it's the first thing I could grab, and you won't always
have time to rummage through a bin. I would've preferred that the
first thing I could grab was a gun." I shrugged. "But here I am with
a fender. What's a fender good for?"

"Not much against a big stick," Heather Davis said.

Heather worked in the laundry with Crystal and another
woman, Becky Moss. Both were in their late twenties or early
thirties and both from New England. Having three people working

in the laundry of a 199-foot yacht might seem outlandish, but when underway, *Ambrosia* required at least five people, usually quite a bit more, depending on the operation. That's twenty-four hours a day and the crew rotates on and off in watches. Through a full day, that's a lot of laundry and bedding.

"That's what you might think," I replied, looping the bitter end of the dock line around my right hand, and then grabbing the fender by its ends. "It's not made for attacking at all. In fact, its name tells you about all it might be good for in a fight. To fend off a strike."

I turned toward Axel. "A nice, slow swing to the head, Axel. Like Casey at the bat."

He moved the boat hook slowly through the air and I raised the fender vertically to head height, still gripping the ends and the line, showing them how it could be used to block.

"One more time," I said to Axel. "But go full speed, like you want to knock my head into the middle of next week."

"Yeah...I don't know about that, Skipper. You could get hurt."

"Don't worry," I said, with a grin. "I won't."

"Well, now you got me worried that I might."

Several of the others laughed.

"You won't get hurt either," I promised. "A level swing to the head, like you were playing baseball and the visiting pitcher just delivered the exact pitch you were hoping for."

Axel planted his feet and held the boat hook up at the ready. When he swung, I took a step forward and brought the fender up quickly. But instead of blocking the end of the hook, the fender met it just past center. The impact on the inflated rubber fender was solid, but fenders are made to absorb the impact of a boat against a dock and bounce it away, so the rebound was just as forceful. The boat hook flew out of Axel's hands, spinning through the air to land several yards away near the surf.

Before he could react, I spun away, flinging the fender out, but keeping hold of the bitter end of the dock line. I whipped around, sending the heavy rubber fender looping around Axel's legs, just behind his knees. The impact of the heavy rubber fender swept him off his feet and he landed on his butt in the sand, legs in the air. He sat up, looked over to where the boat hook had landed, then down at the fender lying at my feet.

I stepped over and extended a hand. "You okay?"

"Yeah," he replied, grabbing my wrist, and pulling himself to his feet. "I was definitely not expecting that."

"Tell the others what it might have felt like if I'd aimed for your head."

He bent over and picked up the fender. It wasn't real heavy, maybe three or four pounds. "I guess just about anything can be a weapon," he said. "If this thing had hit my head, I probably wouldn't be getting up for a while."

"If ever," I added. "A sudden impact to the side of the head from a heavy object, especially one designed to absorb it and push back, could easily break someone's neck or cause a traumatic brain injury."

I nodded to Axel. "Hurry and get the boat hook before it drifts away." Then I turned toward the rest of the group. "The rest of you, turn around and run to the top of the dune and find anything you can use as a weapon. You have sixty seconds. Go!"

Everyone scattered inland. I knew there would be a lot of rocks and sticks. There were two very small volcanic cones on the island and one of them—Pumpkin Hill—wasn't far from where we were. Most of the island was covered in basaltic rocks. Depending on how the basalt formed, the rocks could be hard and denser than granite, or lightweight, full of air bubbles, and crumbly. Small, heavier rocks were more effective as a weapon, but most people will only use it once—as a missile.

"Did I hear you send them off looking for weapons?" Axel asked, as he trotted up with the boat hook.

"Sure did," I said. "And I'll bet Crystal will come back with a pair of equal length sticks."

"Why would you say that?"

Axel and Crystal had been seeing each other for some time, as had Ross and Kassandra. But Crystal apparently hadn't told anyone about her skills. Not even Axel.

"I'm guessing you convinced her to take part in all this," I said.

"Well, yeah. She's a small woman—an easy mark for someone who wants to hurt people."

"She's not such an easy mark as you might think," I said, leaving him bewildered as the others came running back.

Just as I'd expected, two of the girls—Heather and Becky—both had rocks in their hands, and Crystal carried a pair of what looked like pickets from a fence.

Emma and Nancy both had short pieces of driftwood, about the size of baseball bats, while Ross and Kassandra each carried longer ones.

I took the boat hook from Axel and worked the wooden end deep into the sand. Then I hung the bowline knot tied to the fender over the tip, so it hung about head level.

"Becky, you're first," I said, motioning her forward. "This is Freddy Fender and he's not a nice man. He wants to hurt you. What do you do?"

There was no response to the name I'd given the fender, which, in a way, made the age gap between me and them seem even wider.

Becky hurled the first rock, which, although it missed the fender, glanced off the wooden shaft and would have hit Freddy's body, probably in the lower torso.

"Hold up," I said, stepping in front of her before she made her next throw. "What if you'd only found just that one rock. If you throw and miss, you're an empty-handed fighter again. Old Freddy here has at least a boat hook, a rubber fender, and a rope."

I motioned her closer. "The good thing about a rock is that it can be used from a distance. But once used, it's no good to you anymore. Let me ask you a personal question. Has a guy ever said or done something that caused you to slap his face?"

"Once," Becky replied a little sheepishly. "A guy I was seeing had too much to drink and—"

"No need for details," I said. "I bet it got his attention, though, didn't it?" She nodded. "But what if it hadn't? And how about if you'd had something in your hand? Could be anything—an ashtray, beer bottle, table lamp, or I don't know, say, maybe a rock? Yeah, I think a smack upside the head would have a whole different outcome if you were holding a *rock* in your hand."

She looked down at the rock, then back up at me. Her brow slowly creased, nostrils flaring, then she stepped right up to Freddy Fender and smacked him on the side of the head as hard as she could with the rock.

Freddy lost his head.

Becky dropped the rock and gasped, covering her mouth.

"You surprised yourself, didn't you?" I asked, putting a hand on her shoulder.

She looked up at me, startled.

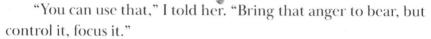

"You can use that," I told her. "Bring that anger to bear, but control it, focus it."

"You made me think of—"

"I know," I said. "And I'm sorry if it hurt to remember." I pulled the boat hook out of the sand and turned to face the rest of the group. "Think outside the box," I said. "Be aware of your surroundings and the situation you're in at all times. Be the one in control. Look each person you pass in the eye. Listen to their footsteps walking away behind you. Note the inanimate objects near you. Think about how things can be used for purposes other than what they were designed for. Above all else, think. Most victims become victims because they panic or let emotion control their action."

"What's the best form of self-defense?" Heather asked.

"That's easy," I replied. "Never allow yourself to be in a position where you have to fight. Walk sure and keep your head on a swivel. The best defense is not looking like an easy target. Thieves and muggers look for certain people. They want to minimize their risk, so they go after those who are smaller and weaker, people who aren't paying attention."

I looked at Crystal and smiled. "Sometimes, the bad guys mistake a person's small size for lack of ability. Crystal, did you tear somebody's fence apart?"

In her hands, she clutched the two pieces of wood horizontally in front of her thighs. "Not really," she replied. "It's missing a lot of pieces. These seemed like the sturdiest."

My swing was lightning fast, bringing the boat hook up in an arcing backhand toward her face. I was ready to stop it inches from her, if she didn't react in time, but she did.

She brought the two fence pickets up, one in each hand. She didn't attempt to block the much heavier boat hook, but easily deflected my strike up and over her head as she arched her back like a limbo dancer and ducked under the blow, before spinning around to face me.

I continued the turn, twirling the short end of the shaft under my extended arm. Then I gripped it in both hands and brought it down in a chopping motion.

Crystal was fast. She danced to the side and attacked. Realizing my swing was another miss, I stepped forward, following the arcing boat hook, and dropping to one knee, raising the shaft in both hands just as Crystal's sticks were coming down toward my head.

The sticks cracked on the hard wooden pole and, rather than twist away to the side, I delayed for just a moment, allowing her to whip the "blades" around the boat hook, stopping just as they made contact with my ribs on either side.

"Whoa," Axel breathed, as Crystal froze in position.

"You're as good as your father said you were," I said quietly.

"*Gracias, mi Capitán,*" she said, as we both stood up. "I haven't had much practice lately."

"What just happened?" Ross asked, looking from me to Crystal.

"My little sister," Kassandra said, putting an arm around the waif's shoulders, "was the Venezuelan women's *juego del garrote* champion two years ago."

"It's called the 'stick game,'" I said. "But it's evolved into much more than a game."

"You never told me this," Axel said, moving closer to her.

Crystal shrugged. "You never gave me reason to. Does it bother you?"

"Bother me?" he asked with a grin. "You're a badass!"

"As you can see," I said to everyone, "nearly any object can be used to attack or defend. And never underestimate the size or age of the person in the fight. Triumph is measured by the size of the fight in the person. Never forget that."

CHAPTER EIGHT

When we returned, Axel and Ross helped me get the tender washed down and put in the garage. Axel kept looking at me in an odd sort of way.

"Something on your mind?" I asked him.

"You knew she was good with those sticks, right?"

"Marcos told me when they first came aboard," I replied. "He said two cartel thugs tried to grab her the night before they fled in Ricardo's boat. She left the two of them unconscious and bleeding in the street."

"How could I not know that?" he asked.

"I don't pretend to understand women, son. But I've been around a lot of warriors, same as you two. The real warriors, those who've been in the shit and survived, don't brag on their accomplishments. You didn't know because you never did anything to warrant her kicking your ass."

"Thank God for that," he said, pulling a strap tight. "Now I just gotta worry about her defending *me*. I could get my man card pulled for something like that."

"Ask her to show you," I said. "It starts out like a choreographed game. You know, like the hand-clapping game kids play? But you use sticks, starting out simple and repetitive, then getting more elaborate, until it looks like you're fencing with dual sabers. It almost looks like a dance."

"You mentioned LINE fighting once," Ross said. "You said it was a mix of several martial arts. What's your favorite?"

I leaned against the tender's gunwale. "Like I said, LINE isn't a real form of self-defense. It's combat fighting and in combat, there's only one outcome—kill or be killed. I've practiced other disciplines over the years. An old friend is a tai chi master, which isn't about fighting at all, but I love the peace and tranquility, the fluid motions, much like tae kwon do. Sort of a dance. But my fallback in a fight is Krav Maga. It's fast, silent, and lethal."

"Like the headbutt you gave that guy in Grenada?" Axel asked.

"Think of an arched bridge," I said. "The curve of the arch transfers the load away from the top in a curve. Your skull has the same shape. Evolution designed us to be able to withstand a powerful blow to the skull without it breaking. Not so much, the bones in the face."

"Are there belts in Krav Maga?" Ross asked. "Like in karate or tae kwon do?"

"Six belts, for those who compete," I replied. "Yellow, orange, green, blue, brown, and black."

"Which do you hold?" Axel asked.

"None. I don't compete."

"But what would you? If you did?"

"Good question," I replied. "I was TAD in Israel for nearly a year with several other NCOs from my recon company. While we were on temporary assignment, we worked with the Egoz Unit of their 89th Infantry Brigade. Egoz is the brigade's reconnaissance unit. The goal was to learn from each other and I spent half my time there, working with their sniper teams and the other half learning their combat fighting. Krav Maga was mostly unheard of outside of those elite Israeli units. When I returned, I taught both LINE and Krav Maga for a few years, so if I were inclined to test, I guess I'd be a black belt in a few disciplines."

"A black belt *and* a sniper," Axel said, as we exited the garage. "Definitely not Captain Hansen."

"You mentioned that once before," I said. "Did you have a problem with Nils?"

"No, sir," Axel replied. "Not at all. Captain Hansen was a fine man and a knowledgeable seaman. I'd cross any ocean in any storm with him in command."

"But that's where his abilities ended," Ross added. "And that's fine because that was just what *Ambrosia* needed. I think what Axel means is, you're that, plus a whole different side."

"I trained and got my license under Nils," I said. "He probably forgot more than I'll ever know."

We went up the side steps to the cockpit, where Matt was sitting at a table with an open book, a bunch of nautical charts, a pad of paper, which he was thumping with a pencil, and a pair of dividers for measuring distance on a chart.

"Got a minute, Cap'n?"

"Thanks for this evening," Ross said.

"Yeah," Axel added. "It was...enlightening."

The two men continued inside, and I sat down with Matt.

"Wasson, mate?" I asked.

He grinned. "It's this bleddy chart plottin', yeah?"

"Ah, studying for your test?"

"It's comin' up right soon," he replied. "I can take the bleddy exam online, so why would they still include something so ancient?"

I grinned at him, recalling one of many simple lessons Tank had explained through action.

"Back when I was a young platoon sergeant," I began. "Tank was my company gunnery sergeant and one day, he was giving a map reading course in the field. GPS was still in its infancy then, but military models were fairly accurate, and the platoon commander had one. I remember that young second lieutenant asking Tank that same question as he spread his map out on the ground, putting a couple rocks on the corners. Tank calmly took the lieutenant's portable GPS from him and placed it on one of the corners, as well. Then he drew his 1911 and put a .45 caliber round through the unit. He calmly picked it up and looked the lieutenant in the eye, saying, 'What you've got now is a paperweight.' Then he picked up the map, noting the small hole in it, and said, 'This is still a map.'"

"How'd that young lieutenant take it?"

"He was one of the good ones," I replied. "He never stopped learning from his older non-comms. He retired as a major general and now works at the Pentagon."

"I get what you're sayin'," Matt said. "But it don't make it easier, yeah?"

I laughed and pointed to his charts. "Try moving from that into the digital age."

"It's just that with all the redundancy aboard, it's a waste of time, innit?"

"You won't always be aboard a boat like this," I said. "One day, you might find yourself putting up the emergency sail in a tender in the middle of the ocean."

"I guess I'd just sail east or west till I ran into something crunchy."

"But it'd sure be easier to sail two hundred miles to Bermuda," I said. "Who's up on the bridge?"

"Val spelled me an hour ago."

"Struggle through it, Matt. If you really can't figure something out, let me know."

I went into the mess hall, then up the spiral staircase to the bridge. Val sat in the navigator's seat, with her feet up on the helmsman's. She had an earbud in one ear and was staring out at the sea.

When she saw me, she quickly sat up, tapped the screen of her cell phone, and removed the earbud. "Good evening, Captain. How'd it go on the beach?"

"Pretty good," I said. "Listening to music?"

She picked up her phone and turned it toward me. "An audiobook," she said. "*The Seven Habits of Highly Effective People.*"

I grinned at her. "I remember you asking me once if Stockwell had an off switch."

She smiled and put the earbud back in as I turned and glanced back into the operations center. Two techs sat in front of glowing screens, each bent over their keyboards, staring intently at their displays. One was Roger Tanaka.

He looked up and started to say something, but I nodded my head toward the inside passageway. He rose from his chair and followed me back to my office, where I closed the hatch.

"Got something?" I asked.

"I checked first to see if anyone within the Armstrong network was working on it. Came up with nothing, although there were a few preliminary notes about how violent most of Honduras had become in the last decade."

"What about the murders?" I asked. "Any connection between the victims?"

"A lot of nothing on linking them," he replied. "Looking at their backgrounds, I found a few who knew one another, went to the same school, or had common contacts. But nothing that tied more than a handful together. And a big zero for anything common to all of them, aside from the obvious—their stance on the environment."

"Were the murders themselves related?"

"I'm convinced they were all murders for hire," he said. "Or at the very least, murders by order. I'm equally sure the Cachiros cartel is behind them. Nearly all of the killings were like the one you showed me—Luna Flores. Two, sometimes three, men with machetes, usually wearing dark hoodies, and almost always in public, like they were sending a message to others, though a few were in their own homes. Four were shot to death. One shooting included four innocent bystanders, killed because they were just sitting in the same cafe."

"How many altogether?"

"Over three hundred in the last twenty years," he replied. "And probably a whole lot more."

As genocide goes, three hundred pales in comparison to the millions of people killed by oppressive regimes throughout history. But environmental activists were such a small part of the world population. Sure, everyone wanted a cleaner planet, but only a small handful actively voiced their concerns and even fewer actually did something.

"Honduras is a dangerous place for the eco-conscious."

"Yes, sir," Roger said. "With your permission, I'd like to dig a little deeper."

"Clear it through New York and open a file," I said.

He nodded and left the office.

Creating a file in the Armstrong database would bring more scrutiny by more people and more computers. It could even result in an operative being assigned to go in and gather more intel. Once enough damning information was accumulated, it would be handed over to the FBI or shared with a foreign government's law enforcement, if they weren't corrupt or actually involved.

When I left my office, I stepped through the exterior hatch onto the side deck. I wanted to collect my thoughts.

The night was cool and crisp. A light breeze blew out of the east and, as my eyes adjusted, thousands of stars began to appear. Aft of the ship sat the tiniest sliver of a crescent moon, dark red and mysterious, riding the horizon like a sailboat running downwind, a puffy spinnaker billowing before it.

In English, Luna Flores translated to flower moon. I wondered if she'd been born in May; the full moon in that month is called the flower moon. The image of the girl's smiling face drifted along with the setting moon. Whoever the man was who'd been cropped out of the picture, I could tell he meant a lot to the girl. Her expression wasn't really one of love or affection, but more like wonder. She idolized the man.

As I stared out across the water, the moon-boat silently sailed over the horizon and was gone.

CHAPTER NINE

The bright off-road driving lights of a black Toyota Land Cruiser pierced the light mist that drifted down from the highlands and settled in the valley. The big SUV forded a small stream, then bulled its way back up onto the rocky road on the other side.

A ramshackle structure overlooking the stream was caught in the bright beams of the SUV's lights. The siding was sullied by the elements, sun-bleached a mottled pale gray. The metal roof was also showing signs of giving way to the elements. Streaks of rust created short, fading lines from each nail and patches of surface rust could be seen where the galvanizing had worn off.

A number of 4x4 trucks and off-road vehicles were parked around the building. Each one, though fairly new, was beaten-up and dirty and had its own story to tell about battling the elements.

The Toyota drove slowly toward the building. Unlike the others, it was pristine and shiny. The bright driving lights clicked off, but the parking lights still illuminated the area in front of it, a pale, orange glow at the front corners and dim red at the back. It stopped in front of a set of sagging steps leading up to a low porch.

The engine and lights were shut off and for a moment, the only sound came from the stream, twenty meters away and three down. Then, a ticking sound started from below the Toyota as the engine and exhaust cooled. Muffled voices could be heard inside, but nothing else.

The front doors opened, shedding no light on the interior, as the driver got out along with a front-seat passenger. Both men were dressed in sturdy clothing, boots, and jackets.

The driver was tall and broad-shouldered. He wore his dark hair long and unkempt, the front and top pulled back in a high ponytail, exposing a wide forehead with many scars. Dark eyes searched the shadows, showing no sign of compassion for anyone or anything.

The other man was shorter and had the physique of a tree stump. His battle-scarred bald head gave way to wide shoulders and a barrel chest. He had quick eyes and a flat nose.

As the dust settled, the two men looked around. Both their jackets bulged under the left arm. They moved in both apposition and concordance, looking all around for anything or anyone that might be a threat. Finally, the driver went to the back door as the shorter man mounted the steps and disappeared inside.

A few seconds passed before he reappeared and nodded at the driver. "Everything is okay, Kennar."

The tall man nodded in return, then opened the back door.

"All is clear, *Jefa*," Kennar said.

A tall, slender woman with long, dark hair and dark features stepped out of the SUV. She was taller than Kennar and it wasn't just due to the heels she wore—they weren't that high. Above them, she wore a modest, gray, knee-length, pencil skirt. She carried a matching jacket over one arm and wore a white silk blouse with the collar open and a loose, pale blue scarf tied below it. If she were anywhere else, most would think she was a businesswoman.

And business was what Paloma Castillo-Cortez was all about.

"Wait outside the door, Geber," she said, striding confidently toward the steps. "Kennar, you're with me."

She quickly ascended the steps and her red-soled heels clicked on the sun-dried planks of the porch.

Kennar following right behind her, knowing from his partner's words that only those who were supposed to be there were inside and there was no danger. In this place, the only danger would be from outside the walls.

Five rough-looking men were inside, one behind the bar, two seated on stools in front of it, and two more at a table. Behind the bartender, a pump shotgun rested on mounts, easily within his reach.

Paloma knew all of them. They all worked for her.

She strolled assertively across the wooden floor, as if she were crossing a conference room to greet a colleague. Kennar walked beside her, half a step back.

The two men at the table rose, chairs scraping across the wood floor.

"*Señora* Castillo-Cortez, thank you for meeting with us," the first man said.

She extended her hand, allowing the two men to gently press their lips to her knuckles.

"I am sure it must be important, Carlos," Paloma responded, taking a seat at their table.

Kennar stood behind her, arms crossed.

"*Si, Señora*," the second man said. "We need your help."

The two men sat back down, and she eyed them both for a moment. "You have found the *hombre gato*, Demian?" she asked in a somewhat condescending tone.

As the *capo* of the Cholóma cartel, Paloma was one of very few women in her position in all of Latin America. She held it because she was smart and ruthless in business. She had contacts all over and received a lot of information.

She looked after her people, creating clinics and schools in some of the poorest regions of the Sula Valley. But everyone in the valley and for some distance beyond knew that it was unwise to cross her. Behind her calm-looking, clerical appearance, she was a vicious woman and more than one of her enemies had learned that the hard way.

"The only time anyone knows where he is," Demian said, "is when he sends one of the great cats to kill our *soldados*. It is getting difficult to find anyone willing to walk the trails at night."

"Does such a man really exist?"

"We are certain he is one of the *indígena*," Carlos said. "He strikes only at night and seems to know a new trail as soon as it is created."

"A man cannot control a jaguar," Paloma said, looking sternly at each man in turn. "Moving through the forest at night is perilous, that's all. You and your *soldados* are paid well for the risk you take."

Carlos looked at the other *teniente*, then back to Paloma. "It is not the money, *Jefa*. We would not ask, if there was anything we could do. After three of the attacks, we have found where the man lay in wait with the jaguar, sending it after our *oficials* when they passed on the trail. He is like a ghost in the forest. We cannot kill what we cannot see."

Paloma considered it a moment. Then she turned and asked over her shoulder, "Has El Astilla returned from Guatemala?"

"He will arrive in San Pedro Sula in the morning," Kennar replied.

El Astilla—The Sliver—was one of Paloma's most trusted *sicarios* or hired hitmen. He was called that because anyone around his victims—their friends, families, or anyone else—would only see a sliver of movement before his target fell dead, laid open by El Astilla's razor- sharp blade.

"El Astilla?" Carlos asked. "I have never even met him."

"Few have and lived to tell about it," Paloma said. "He will contact you. His method may be unorthodox. Don't expect him to walk in here as I did."

"Do you think he can find this man?"

Paloma stood and slowly smoothed her hands over her skirt. The two men rose with her.

"If such a man exists, El Astilla will find him," Paloma said, a slight smile parting her full lips. "And when he does, he will fillet his body in the streets of Cholóma."

CHAPTER TEN

The image of the girl's body lying covered in the street came to my mind. A life cut short, only because she cared about the world she lived in. No, that wasn't true. She was cut down in the prime of life because she had the temerity to speak out about it.

I turned and went back inside, then opened the hatch to my quarters, located at the aft end of the upper deck.

"Out here," Savannah called.

I looked out on the terrace and saw my wife and our son sitting under the overhang with Kassandra, Marcos, and Grady Lawson. It was getting late, and I was tired. I didn't feel much like socializing.

"What's going on?" I asked. "Trouble in the galley?"

"Oh, no *Capitán*," Marcos said. "We are planning a *celebracion*."

"It's Matt's birthday in three days," Savannah said. "I thought we could surprise him with something special for dinner."

I looked at the two men, one a chef from a five-star resort in Maracaibo, Venezuela and the other, a soul-food chef from downtown Atlanta.

"Either of you know any Cornish dishes?"

"Not really," Grady said. "I'm not even sure where Cornwall is. Most of the dishes I looked up seem to include seafood, so I'm guessing it's on the coast of England."

"Cornwall is a rocky peninsula sticking way out into the North Atlantic," I said. "Everything there revolves around the sea. But you're not likely to catch any turbot or cod in these waters."

"We have plenty of snapper, though," Kassandra said. "Brined, it'd make a decent substitute. The rest is all about preparation."

"Not if we make the Cornish fish stew," Marcos said, as I sat down beside Savannah. He looked over at me. "That is what we decided."

"Fish stew?"

"It's like...comfort food for Cornish folk," Grady said.

Marcos nodded. "But it includes snails, shellfish, and squid."

"There are clams here," Savannah said. "Finn's been finding them. And I've seen some mussels, too. But I don't know if they're edible."

"I can find out," Alberto said, sitting on the deck, petting Finn.

"There are many land snails in Venezuela that can be eaten," Marcos suggested.

Alberto got up and came over to the table with his small tablet. "I can find that out, too. The best ones to catch, even."

"Then all we have to do," I said, "is collect enough snails, clams, and mussels to feed forty people and hope we don't poison them all."

"Here," Alberto said, squeezing in between me and Savannah. "These are called apple snails."

"*Excelente*," Marcos said. "We have them in Venezuela. But they are very big there, as large as a man's fist."

Alberto shrugged. "Cut 'em up."

The two cooks looked at each other.

"Ain't no reason they gotta be served in the shell," Grady said, leaning over the table to look at the picture on Alberto's tablet. "Hey, I saw a bunch of those along the edge of the lagoon."

"I will organize a clam hunt," Kassandra said.

"Take Alberto and Finn with you," Savannah said. "He can find them in the water."

Kassandra turned toward Alberto and smiled down at him. "How?"

"Not me," he said, his face flushing. "Our dog. Finn dives for them all the time."

"Well, this is something I must see," Kassandra said. "Will you and Finn show me and Ross where to find clams?"

"Sure," Alberto replied enthusiastically.

"Mayra and I can find the mussels," Marcos said. "I know the best ones."

"Catching edible squid's gonna be a problem," I said. "But if you can substitute conch, there are plenty of those around."

Grady thought for a moment. "Yeah, I think I can do that. I'll let the divers know to catch a few." He looked at Marcos. "Think ten or twelve oughta do it?"

"I think it will work," Marcos agreed, then turned toward Savannah. "What goes in will be different, but I think we can make it look and taste very close."

"And you plan to surprise Matt with all this?" I asked. "He's a pretty observant guy."

"Val said she could keep him busy," Savannah said.

"What do you need me to do?" I asked.

Savannah patted my hand. "Nothing at all, Jesse. Too many cooks spoil the broth."

"Speakin' of things gettin' spoilt," Grady said, rising from the table. "I gotta get back down to the kitchen."

Marcos got up with him. "I must go find Mayra," he said. "Come, Kassandra. We have much planning to do."

I walked our guests to the hatch as Savannah herded Alberto into his room, along with Finn, to get showered and ready for bed. Finally, the two of us were alone.

"Sorry about that," she said, taking a wine glass from the hanging rack and waggling it at me. I nodded, and she took down a second one. "But I used to love helping Mother plan parties and I often went to great lengths to surprise Flo when it was just the two of us on the boat."

We went back out onto the terrace and sat in the double lounge chair, open to the sky above us. After she poured the wine and we stretched out together, I could feel the warmth of her hip through my cargo shorts.

"It's been nice just hanging out here," she said. "But you seem a little itchy to get moving again."

I'd been trying hard to shut down these last few days. Despite our fine accommodations, I was starting to get a feeling for home, my thoughts drifting to my little island in the Content Keys as I relaxed on the sand or hovered above a colorful reef.

"I seem itchy?" I asked, genuinely confused about how she could read that in my behavior. "What in the world makes you say that?"

"I know you, Jesse. Sometimes better than you know yourself."

"Come on. I've been doing nothing but relaxing and winding down. Just what the doctor ordered."

She took a sip of wine and nodded. "For the most part. But you were uptight for a while after you spoke to that Honduran Navy officer."

"He told me some troubling news, that's all."

"Uh-huh," she said, staring up at the sky. "And you're not planning something already with Roger?"

"He's bored," I said, blowing it off with a forced chuckle. "All I did was give the guy something—"

"After all you and I have been through?" she asked, her voice sharp, but her eyes still on the heavens. "Don't you even *think* about going back to lying to protect me, Jesse McDermitt."

Full name—DEFCON Two, I thought, as I stared at the side of her face.

I sat back, defeated. "Something's going on that I don't like."

"None of us do. So, why's this one so troubling for you?"

Just then, the door slid open, and Alberto and Finn came out.

"I'm going to bed now," he said. "But Finn was scratching to go out."

"I'll take him down," I said.

He hugged us both and went back inside as Finn did his familiar circling routine before lying down next to me.

"What's up with you?" I asked, reaching down to pet his neck and shoulders.

"Going 'out' doesn't always mean the bathroom for dogs," Savannah said. "Woden always liked to be outside. Unless it was raining."

I laughed, remembering how he reacted to downpours. "He surely didn't like getting rained on."

Finn sat up and laid his head across my thigh, so I could stroke the fur between his eyes with my thumb. His ears fell back, and his eyes half closed in total relaxation.

"I guess he's just wanting some adult attention," I said. "He's an old man and Alberto's hard to keep up with."

"Tell me what's bothering you," Savannah said. "What's going on?"

"Wild animals are being caught or killed," I said. "Endangered species; sold on the black market. When the forest is empty, they cut down endangered trees and sell the wood on the black market, too. Then they send in farmers to grow coca where several acres of forest used to be."

Finn whined, turning his big golden-brown eyes up at me. His yellow fur was turning white around his eyes, on his chin, and along his mouth.

"Don't worry, buddy," I said, and resumed stroking with my thumb. "I won't let anyone get you."

Finn doesn't worry about Finn," Savannah said. "Woden never worried about himself either. His whine was to let you know he feels the same way you do. And so do I."

"Be careful with those thoughts," I warned them both. "They could get you killed around here."

CHAPTER ELEVEN

Early the next morning, before sunrise, I went up to the bridge to relieve Kris Carter. He was the second helmsman to Axel and had been aboard *Ambrosia* only a few months longer than I had.

Kris was a serious young man most of the time—quiet and easy to get along with. The Caribbean was a long way from his hometown of Johnson City, in East Tennessee.

Even while *Ambrosia* was off duty and anchored, I wanted one person on the bridge and alert at all times. If nothing else, just to answer the phone. With eight of us in the bridge crew, we rotated two hours on and fourteen off while the ship was off duty. But over the last several days in the Bay Islands, the schedule had become lax and the bridge crew swapped watches often. A few times, when I had nothing else to do, I just went up and took a watch from whoever was there.

When we were underway, our watch schedules were longer and the extended periods with four on the bridge at all times were demanding, so we took advantage of downtime as much as possible, while still maintaining control at all times.

"Morning, Kris," I said, stepping through the hatch.

"I figured you'd be a might early," he said, starting to rise.

I held up a hand as I headed toward the coffee maker. "Don't get up. Anything going on?"

"A whole lot of nothin'," he replied. "Ain't even seen a fish jump out there in the water."

I carried my coffee over to the port counter and leaned on it, looking out over the foredeck. "Boring, huh?"

"Not so much," he said. "It sure beats watchin' the dough rise in Mee-maw's kitchen. But the fun part's just about to start."

I looked at the digital clock set in the overhead console—0602.

When I looked back at the eastern horizon, the first bright part of the sun peeked over it. I took my shades out of my pocket and put them on. In minutes, the bridge, foredeck, and the waters around us were bathed in natural light as dawn quickly heralded a new day.

Sunrise and sunset look totally different. I don't know why, but sunsets are usually bathed in pastel colors of red and orange while sunrises are almost always bright yellow and white-hot light. This day was no exception, as the sun rose up above the horizon and began to climb into a bright blue sky.

"I see you up here a lot on the morning watch," I said.

He took a sip of his coffee and nodded. "Nobody likes the four to six and six to eight watches," he said. "I guess I turn in earlier than most. So, the last coupla days, I traded off with anyone who wanted to sleep in. I like to sit here and think when it's quiet and the sun's just a-coming up out of the ocean."

"What made you want to work and live on a boat?" I asked, just making conversation.

He glanced over his mug at me. "Not a lot of gay farmers in East Tennessee, and I wasn't included in a lot of things. So, it was here or Nash-vegas."

"Not a lot of gay guys here, either."

"True enough," he agreed. "But the crew here, and really, all of

78

Armstrong, has been very accepting. It's not like it's contagious or anything."

He went over to the small sink and washed his mug. "Well, if I'm gonna catch that first dive boat, I best get a move on."

"Oh, hey," I said, stopping him at the hatch. "Let everyone know to keep an eye open for conchs. The galley needs at least a dozen for the evening meal in two days for Matt's birthday. So, tell them to keep it on the down low."

"Will do, Captain," he replied, pulling the hatch open. "You have a good-un."

I sat down at the helm and out of habit, picked up the bridge Metis tablet.

In Greek mythology, Metis was a Titan-goddess of good counsel, planning, cunning, and wisdom. Aboard *Ambrosia*, those five letters only meant one thing: the Multi-Encrypted Technical Interface System that connected all of Armstrong's computers and devices, as well as the ship itself. From the Metis tablet, I could access any console or control on the ship and access the vast Armstrong computer network.

I scrolled through the last few ship's log entries. There were only two in the last twenty-four hours. A sailboat anchored a mile away, shortly after sunset, and left forty minutes before I got to the bridge.

My personal satellite phone vibrated in my pocket, emitting a soft trill. When I took it out, the display showed it was a number with a Honduran prefix.

I stabbed the *Accept* button. "McDermitt."

"This is Jorge Flores."

"What can I do for you, Ensign?"

"I am on Utila. Are you still in the area?"

I was certain that if he wanted to know our location, he could easily get it, but I played along. "Haven't moved since I saw you yesterday."

"Are you available? I have a man with me who would like very much to meet you."

"Who is it?" I asked, picking up the binos and scanning the beach in both directions.

"I would rather not say, *Capitán.*"

"And both of you are on Utila now?" I asked, satisfied that there wasn't anyone watching *Ambrosia* from shore.

"*Si, Capitán.* Will you meet with us?"

"Can you come here?" I asked. "I just started my watch on the bridge."

"It would be better here," Jorge said. "Do you know a place called Rockies on Pumpkin Hill Beach?"

I looked east through the binoculars. Pumpkin Hill Beach was five miles away, just around the point, and close to the horizon. I couldn't see anything in the water off the beach.

"It'll take me twenty minutes to get there," I said.

"We will see you then," Jorge said and ended the call.

I opened the photo app and then the picture of Luna Flores, Jorge's sister. It was obviously a snapshot, maybe taken by a close friend, or even Jorge himself. I didn't think it was him who was cropped out of the picture, unless Luna was unusually small. Jorge wasn't tall, maybe five-six or five-seven. From the angle of the man's arm behind her, he was at least eight or nine inches taller than her. If she were average height, he was likely six feet tall.

Her eyes haunted me for some reason. The photo was taken from directly in front of her, but her face was turned slightly to her right, looking up at the man, as if she were hanging on his every word.

I put my phone in my pocket, then pulled up the current day's watch schedule on the Metis. Val McLarin had the next watch, so I punched her cabin number into the ship's intercom and pushed the button. She answered almost immediately. "Yeoman McLarin."

"It's Jesse," I said. "Sorry to bother you. Is there any way you can take over on watch? I have to go somewhere. I doubt I'll be long and will take your watch at zero eight hundred."

"I'll be there in just a few minutes," she replied.

I thanked her, left the bridge, and went back to my quarters.

"What are you doing back?" Savannah asked, sitting at the dinette with Alberto, a book open between them.

"I have to go check something out," I said, disappearing into our bedroom. "Val's on her way up to take over."

I opened my little sock drawer and took out my new Sig Sauer P320, already in its holster. Tank had given me the new M18 variant, which the Marine Corps had just adopted to replace the Beretta M9 sidearm as standard issue.

I withdrew it from its holster, switched the safety off, and pulled the slide back slightly, press-checking the weapon to see the round in the chamber. Returning it to safe position, I reinserted the weapon in the holster and clipped it to my waist.

In the mirror, I adjusted my shirt over it, so the bulky 9mm handgun, loaded with eighteen rounds of hollow-point ammunition, was barely visible.

I took a loaded spare magazine out of the drawer and put it in my left pocket to balance the load.

"What is it you need to check on?" Savannah asked from the doorway, watching me.

By now, she was used to seeing me carry whenever we went anywhere. My philosophy, taught to me by both my dad and my grandfather, was that it was far better to have something and not need it, than to need it and not have it. So, I carried a weapon wherever I went. Except aboard *Ambrosia.*

I looked past Savannah. Alberto was still sitting at the table, writing. "I'm meeting Ensign Flores and another man at Pumpkin Hill Beach."

"And you don't know who the other man is?"

"I think it has something to do with Flores's sister's murder."

We'd remained out on the terrace the night before, and I'd told her about Luna Flores and the other murder victims, as well as the discussion I'd had with the ensign.

"You don't trust him?" she asked, glancing down at my waist.

"I don't know him," I replied. "Trust comes through getting to know someone."

"You be careful," she said, kissing me on the cheek, as if I were heading off to the office in rush-hour traffic.

"Are we still going to the beach?" Alberto asked, as I came back into the living room.

"As soon as we can," I said. "But I have to swap watches with Val so I can go do something important right now. But we'll be on the beach shortly after ten hundred."

"Roger that," he said, then went back to his studies.

I ruffled his hair and kissed Savannah, then headed back up to the bridge. At the intercom, I buzzed the garage.

"Equipment room. Antonio Giuseppe."

"It's Captain McDermitt," I said, as Val and Matt came in. "Please put one of the PWCs in the water for me."

"Right away, sir." Antonio replied.

"Goin' somewhere, Cap'n?" Matt asked.

"I just got off the phone with that Honduran Navy ensign," I replied. "He wants me to meet someone."

Val lifted the side of my shirt and whistled. "That the new one?"

"Never whistle on a boat," Matt cautioned her. "To whistle is to challenge the wind and she might blow up a proper gale."

"Another Cornish superstition?" she asked him.

"Superstitions are based on cause and effect," I said, then nodded at Matt. "It's always best to not tempt the gods."

Val pointed again at the sidearm. "An abundance of caution?"

"It was a gift from Tank," I said. "The new Sig the Marine Corps just adopted."

Roger Tanaka came out of the op center. He hadn't been there when I'd come up to relieve Kris.

"I found out something interesting about Miss Flores," Roger said. "Sorry, couldn't help but overhear."

"I don't know who it is with Ensign Flores or what they want," I said to Val, then turned to Roger. "What'd you find out?"

"Her brother might have downplayed her activism," Roger said. "She was a highly intelligent, well-educated woman, with double PhDs in ecology and evolutionary biology."

"So, not just a local tree-hugger?" I asked. "No slight intended."

"She *was* local," he replied. "But she received her doctorates from Harvard and studied under some of the best minds in the field, including the famed South American wildlife biologist, Professor Mejia, who once lived in La Ceiba, where the murder took place."

"The plot thickens," I said. "I'll try to find out why he hadn't mentioned her creds earlier and see what else I can learn."

"Don't worry about the next watch," Val said. "I was going to help Matt study all morning anyway. We can do that anywhere."

"Thanks," I said. "I still owe you one."

"And one day," she said with a smile, "I'll collect."

CHAPTER TWELVE

Down on the big work deck at *Ambrosia's* stern, Antonio was tying off a Sea-Doo GTS to the recessed stern cleat.

"I thought you didn't like these things, Captain," Antonio said, handing me a life vest.

"I don't like the way most folks use them," I replied, buckling on the low-profile vest.

"I agree with you there," Antonio said. "But this boat's not the MacArthur Causeway and we're not on Biscayne Bay, so you won't have any trouble. Ever ridden one?"

Antonio Giuseppe was from Miami. His parents had moved there from the Bronx when he was a kid, but he still had some of that New York Italian accent.

"No," I replied, looking over the controls. "Looks simple enough. Finger throttle kind of like the front brake on a bike."

"And on the left side," Antonio said, pointing out another lever control, "this isn't a clutch. The Sea-Doo has brakes. It really just reverses the direction of the water jet, so be careful. If you're wide open and hit the brake, it'll stop really fast."

"I'll keep that in mind."

He pulled the Sea-Doo alongside the platform and held up a clip attached to a coiled lanyard. "This is the key. It's electronic and clips onto this little ball under the steering." He pointed it out and handed me the key. "Always keep the other end clipped to you, and if ya fall off, the Doo will stop dead in the water.

"Both of our PWCs are set to economy mode," he continued, pointing at a touch pad on the left side. "You can control that here, but she'll still go like a bat outta hell even in eco mode. Now, in *sport* mode, it'll be like the bats are being chased by banshees."

"Banshees outta hell," I said with a nod. "Got it."

"Right here in front of the seat," he said, pointing to a spot under the console, "there's a release to raise this whole top section." There was a click and Antonio raised the console and handlebars. "Inside here are extra life vests, dock lines, and this."

He pulled out a bright-yellow, plastic auger-looking thing.

"What's that?" I asked.

"It's a sand auger for a beach umbrella," he replied. "They make great anchors for the ski. There's two of them in each Sea-Doo, to anchor fore and aft."

He put the makeshift anchor back inside and closed the lid, then pointed out the obvious. "This red button here starts it and it'll always start in neutral, but even in neutral, it'll creep forward 'cause the impeller's always engaged. The jets are just redirected to the sides in neutral. If you turn the steering while you're in neutral, it'll pivot around. Tap the throttle and the jets open up for forward, idling about two miles per hour. Hold the brake and the jets are directed for reverse. If you give it a little gas while holding the brake, it'll back up faster. Let off the brake and mash the throttle and off you go."

I thanked him, secured the "dead-man" cord to my vest, climbed on, and clipped the key in place. There was an audible beep, and the dash came on, telling me the tank was full. I hit the starter button and the engine jumped to life under my seat.

Antonio untied the line and pushed the Sea-Doo away from the platform. "Just like riding a bike, Skipper. Be careful."

I nodded and turned the "handlebars" to the left. The back of the machine swung away, pointing the nose back toward the platform. I held the brake and brought the steering back to the center, and the Sea-Doo slowly backed away from the ship.

Releasing the brake, I turned to the right and waited for the nose to come around, clearing the platform, then gave it a little gas.

The response was quick as the machine dug in and lurched forward at about five knots. I squeezed the throttle a little more and moved the steering back and forth, getting a feel for how it maneuvered at low speed. I quickly found that, like riding a bicycle, I had to lean into the turns.

Feeling more confident, I throttled up and the Sea-Doo climbed over its bow wave and started planing across the water. In seconds, the digital speedometer said I was going thirty-five miles per hour. It felt a good deal faster, sitting just a foot above the water.

The steering was a lot touchier than at low speed, which I expected. Soon, I got the sense that I actually was riding a motorcycle—riding on a bumpy road through rolling hills.

I kept the PWC in deeper water, well away from the beach, to avoid the dive sites. The waves were coming at a bit of an angle, but they were relatively small. I increased speed a little, standing slightly to absorb the bumps and lessen the bounce when I went over a wave.

By the time I was halfway to Pumpkin Hill Beach, I felt quite comfortable and made a few high-speed turns. Just getting the feel of it, I told myself. But the truth was, it was fun, and I didn't do a lot of things just for the fun of it anymore.

Pumpkin Hill was visible from just about anywhere on the water. As hills go, it wasn't very high, only 243 feet above sea level, but most of the island was flat, and the hill was one of several volcanic cones on its eastern end.

In my mind's eye, I could see the little island growing out of the sea. As it emerged, the easterly trade winds would have blown ash and dust toward the west. It'd probably settled on the sea mount's underwater western slope, building the island slowly over time. Wind-driven wave action would have caused erosion on the east end, as waves would wrap around the island, moving more sediment to the west end.

Half a mile off the beach, I turned and headed toward shore, scanning the beach. There were two boats pulled up on the sand and two men were leaning against one of them. As I got closer, I recognized one of them as Jorge Flores. He wasn't in uniform.

I angled toward their boat, bringing the Sea-Doo down off plane and creeping forward. I could feel the weight of the Sig on my right hip, and checked to make sure my shirt covered it.

The man with Jorge was older. He was dark-skinned, had a wide nose, a thin beard, and unkempt, graying hair. He looked more like a South Pacific islander than the Native Americans in the States. His build was slight, but he was tall—very tall, if he was from one of the native tribes of Central America. Their people were usually very short in stature. He was dressed in ragged clothes, a wide-brimmed hat, and his feet were bare.

To keep from sucking sand into the impeller, I killed the engine, then coasted another five feet until it gently nudged the sandy shore.

Jorge nodded. "We can talk out here, if you don't mind."

"Not at all," I said, stepping off and pulling the Sea-Doo higher on the sand.

"Captain McDermitt, this is Professor Mejia, a world-renowned—"

"Harvard professor and wildlife biologist," I said, cutting him off, and extending a hand. "Pleased to meet you, Professor. I've heard of you and your work."

I hadn't until half an hour ago, but keeping others off balance was one of my stocks-in-trade. I wasn't Captain McDermitt at that moment. I was on a recon mission, far from home, and all alone.

His grip was firm and dry, fingers and palm calloused. A working man's hand. He had deep lines around sad-looking brown eyes, and I got the impression that he was a true working professor, a man with an analytical mind and strong muscles, who got down in the trenches to gather data from old bones and clay pots.

"Jorge has told me much about you and your organization as well, Captain."

"Please, just call me Jesse."

"Then you must call me Aldrick," he said.

CHAPTER THIRTEEN

It turned out that Aldrick Mejia was Jorge and Luna Flores's uncle. He and his sister—their mother—were from a small tribe who'd inhabited the Río Plátano area for millennia. His people had lived deep in the jungle, overlooked by explorers and modern society until early in the twentieth century.

"I am Tawahka," Aldrick said. "Our people number less than three thousand today."

Having a naturally curious mind, I knew a little about the indigenous peoples of the Americas. But I'd never heard of the Tawahka. He went on to tell me about his people and others in Central America. His wealth of knowledge amazed me.

"You went from being part of a nearly extinct hunter-gatherer tribe in the rainforest to becoming a professor at one of the world's most prestigious universities. That's quite an accomplishment."

"Not really," he replied, his voice showing almost no trace of any sort of accent. "I am sixty years old. I was found by Peace Corps members when I was about four, alone in the jungle. I'd become separated from my troupe and was nearly dead. I learned later that my parents died after visiting a modern village, most likely from a virus. Much later, just a few years ago, in fact, I found I had siblings."

"As a four-year-old, you survived on your own?" I asked.

"I was very small," he replied. "And very near death. I only know what the woman who took me in told me. I do not even know my own birthday."

"This Peace Corps woman?" I asked. "She raised you?"

"Yes," he replied. "Her family was wealthy. She saw that I received an education. But a part of me was still in the forest. I knew what was coming for my people and the only way to save them was to become better educated in the ways of the world. For most of my people, the world beyond the rainforest brought only death and misery."

"Is she still alive?"

"The woman who raised me?" he asked. I nodded. "Yes, she is eighty-five and lives in a grand house with many people to take care of her."

"Do you miss your former way of life?"

"I only remember parts of it." Then he grinned. "Air-conditioning is a comfort. Advanced medicine is essential. Very old men among my people are only in their fifties."

"How did you become separated from your family?" I asked, very curious.

"It is different in the forest," he began. "It is a very unforgiving place. Defenseless young, be they a deer or a child, rarely survive more than a few hours. I'm sure my parents and the rest of the troupe searched for me, but once darkness fell, they would have given up."

"Just given up?"

"The forest is not like the city," he replied. "A living thing the size of a small boy is nothing more than sustenance for the predators of the jungle. It would have been pointless after the darkness came."

"This troupe?" I asked. "They—you—lived wild in the forest, not in a village or something?"

"The Tawahka were forest nomads since the beginning of time," he explained. "But by the 1980s most of my people had settled into villages in the Río Plátano Biosphere Reserve. By then, I was in college."

"Did you ever return?"

"I have only gone to the village my parents died at a few times. You might say I had a voracious appetite for learning. I remember enjoying being alone. Even as a child, I learned on my own, studying the ways of the forest and remembering everything I witnessed. The mind of a child is like a dry sponge."

"My grandfather often said the same thing."

He nodded toward his nephew, who'd moved away from us while Aldrick talked of his people. "Jorge is Tawahka, as were both his parents, and theirs before them. Only in recent times have I learned that I had a brother and sister and that her husband left the village when Luna was an infant. I only learned of my niece and nephew two years ago. I spoke at one of her commencements and she approached me afterward, telling me of her family and their names."

I glanced over at Jorge, suddenly realizing what his sister's death meant.

Worldwide, about thirty percent of the population were between the ages of fifteen and thirty-five and a little over half of those were women. In a cross-section of three thousand people who were not of mixed ancestry, there were likely only a few hundred women of reproductive age. The loss of even one in that small of a group could mean the tipping point toward extinction. We tend to think of that term as it relates to dinosaurs and other animals, but thousands of human races have also become extinct.

"Is Jorge married?" I asked.

The sad eyes grew sadder. "No," he replied. "And he has no children."

"I think I understand your loss," I said. "And I don't mean that in just a personal way. Were you close with Luna?"

"One of my best students," he said, his eyes suddenly sparkling. "She reminded me a lot of myself when I was young. Did you know she earned a doctorate in evolutionary biology? Her thesis was on the possibility of stopping extinction through DNA research."

"That didn't go over so well at *Jurassic Park*," I said. "But I get the idea she was thinking more about her own people."

He laughed. "No, we're a long way from creating dinosaur clones, but there is anonymous surrogacy for women unable to conceive. Through DNA research and in vitro fertilization, her hypothesis is solid. But only if enough people of pure blood are willing to take part as donors."

"Was that what she was working on in La Ceiba when she was killed?"

"Surrogacy? No. Her work in the city was more about environmental issues. She often spoke out publicly against the cartels and the government for the nonstop cutting of the rainforest and the killing of its inhabitants."

Digging my phone out, I pulled up the image of Luna Flores and showed it to him.

He took my phone and smiled as a tear ran down his cheek.

"That was taken the evening we first truly met, when she received her PhD in ecology." He pulled his hair back from his face, gripping it on top of his head for a moment. "I was in the photo, too.

Her friend took it and afterward Luna spoke to me in our own language. She told me who her parents were and I realized she was my niece. We talked well into the night, as if nobody else was around." He handed the phone back and smiled. "One of my colleagues pulled me aside and expressed his concern that I was spending too much time with a female student. I was flattered, in a way."

I chuckled, looking down at her. "She was a beautiful woman. When I saw her picture, I was drawn. I don't know why. Maybe because I have three daughters of my own. But I never gave thought to any of them being the linchpin of a whole race."

"Jorge tells me you may be able to help," Aldrick said.

"Help stop the extinction of a people?"

His eyes saddened again. "It is probably too late to stop that," he said. "I would settle for help in stopping the destruction of the habitat that created us."

Later, when I got back aboard *Ambrosia*, my thoughts were on just how fragile life was. A traffic accident could take out a whole family, eliminating any future generations. A guy named Tank could have followed orders and remained on the helicopter, and a dozen men might have died, ending any chance for their genes to be passed on.

Still, the human race would continue.

But what about something that decimated a whole race, like Hitler tried to do? He wasn't the first. Genocide has occurred all over the world. Just in the last century, aboriginal people in Australia were nearly wiped out and the Ache people in Paraguay were hunted down as recently as 1970, with government-sanctioned raiding parties killing the men and enslaving the women and children.

I remembered when I was about twelve, a story on the front page of the New York Times confused me. I'd been living with my grandparents, Mam and Pap, for four years by then. So, I asked Pap about the story that said slaves were being sold in a country called Paraguay.

Many parents and grandparents would gloss over tough questions like that in a misguided attempt to protect a child's innocence. But Pap called that intentional ignorance. He always said the only dumb questions were those you didn't ask.

Instead, Pap read the story with me, though I knew he'd read it previously. He'd subscribed to the Times ever since he returned from the Pacific after WWII. He read every issue, cover to cover, every article, photo caption, stock index, advertisements, sports, the whole thing.

"Just because somebody's different from you," he'd told me, "it doesn't mean they're inferior or superior to you."

He went on to explain that there were people in the world who thought of those who lived a more primitive lifestyle as nothing more than naked savages, incapable of anything requiring intelligence.

He'd gone on to tell me about some of the people he'd met on far-flung islands in the Pacific and how they'd lived in a manner we'd consider primitive—much like the Ache people in the news story. But he said they didn't care at all about our technology and were very happy just living off the land, the rivers, and the sea.

I could totally relate to that.

"Who was it Ensign Flores wanted you to meet?" Savannah asked, when I got back to our quarters.

"His uncle," I replied. "I'll tell you all about it when we get to the beach."

"Yeah, about that," she said. "Both tenders are out with divers."

"Not a problem," I told her. "For such a short run, we can take one of the Sea-Doos."

CHAPTER FOURTEEN

"I thought you hated those things," Savannah said, as we sat down on the couch.

"It's a machine," I replied. "An inanimate object. On its own, it's incapable of doing anything. It's just that usually when I see one, the operator is doing really stupid stuff."

"Alberto took Finn to the grass," she said. "All three of us can't ride on one of those *things*, can we?"

"Yeah, but I don't think we can include Finn."

"Include Finn in what?" Alberto asked, coming through the hatch, Finn right behind him.

"We have to take one of the PWCs to the beach," I told him.

"Cool! I like riding on them!"

Alberto had ridden on them with Antonio and Ross in the Med last month, while we were anchored off Cadiz, Spain, waiting for a storm over the Eastern Atlantic to clear out.

"No room for all three of us and Finn, too," I said

"Aw, he was looking forward to it," Alberto said, sitting cross-legged on the floor.

Finn sat next to him, looking at me and Savannah.

"He was, huh?" I asked.

Alberto put an arm around Finn. "He likes the beach. He told me."

"Wait," I said, remembering last night. "Weren't you and he going to go with Ross and Kassandra?"

"They're on the beach already," Savannah said. "They had one of the dive groups drop them off early this morning. Alberto wanted to wait until you got back."

I got up and slapped my thigh, getting Finn's attention. "You wanna go for a ride on a Sea-Doo, buddy?"

Finn stood, his big tail slapping his flanks. At twelve years old, the word "go" still got him as excited as it did when he was a pup.

"What are you going to do?" Savannah asked.

"I'll take Finn and Alberto to shore and drop them off with Ross and Kassandra," I replied, heading into our room, and putting my Sig and spare mag away. "That'll give you time to change before I come back and get you."

With that decided, Alberto and Finn went with me down to the platform where I'd left the PWC tied up. I was already wearing board shorts, and Alberto had his on when we ate breakfast. Finn was always ready to get wet.

"I'll get on first," I said. "You'll sit behind me, all the way on the back, and hold onto my belt, okay?"

"What about Finn?"

"I'll have him sit on my lap with his front paws on the front of the seat. With my arms around him, he won't fall off."

We managed to get on without tumbling in the water, and I started the engine and let go of the line. Finn wasn't a stranger to boats or the water. He knew to always stay in one place. He'd ridden all kinds of watercraft and seemed to sense the smaller ones were more susceptible to movement from its occupants, so he sat still while I got the thing moving, then turned his head and licked my chin for good luck.

I kept the speed down, never getting on plane, and we headed to the beach. The Sea-Doo is designed for three passengers, but I don't think they ever figured one of them being a dog.

Seeing Ross and Kassandra walking along the shore, I turned and headed toward them.

"Go faster, Dad," Alberto called from behind me, his fists gripping my belt tightly.

I wondered how many men had heard that demand from a young boy and not responded by stepping on the gas a little.

Pulling the throttle lever slightly caused the Sea-Doo to gain speed and slowly rise up on plane. Once we were slippery, I increased speed a little more.

Finn barked and Alberto yelled with glee, but both stayed put.

The ride was short, and I slowed as we neared the beach. Ross waded out to knee-deep water to help and to show me the depth. I tapped the brake, putting the machine in neutral, idling forward, then killed the engine when we were ten feet from him.

Finn took that as his cue and started squirming. Rather than try to lift him off, I just raised my hands from the handlebars, and he jumped into the water.

Being a Lab, Finn had a dense undercoat of fur that trapped air, allowing him to float easier as well as remain warm in colder water. He used his big, thick tail as a rudder as he swam in circles, waiting for Alberto.

"We were about to give up on you," Ross said, easily lifting the boy off and putting him down in the water. "We haven't found a single clam."

"Get us some clams, Finn," I said.

His ears and head came up higher and he turned toward shore, webbed feet churning at full speed. Clams were about Finn's favorite treat and some places we'd visited lately hadn't had any.

I turned back to Ross. "I have to run back and get Savannah. Don't worry— if there's a clam anywhere around here, Finn can find it. You might have to swim out and dive with him when he finds a good bed."

"What?" Kassandra asked. "He doesn't find them in the shallows?"

"Finn taught himself to find clams when he was a pup," I replied. "He's from the same place as Savannah—the South Carolina Lowcountry. The tide can rise and fall ten feet there and clams exposed by the tides aren't as good as those from deeper water." I turned back to Ross. "Watch his nose when he dives. His body might twist and turn, but his nose will be pointed at his target."

"This I gotta see," Ross said, putting a hand on Alberto's shoulder and leading him after Finn, who was already wading ashore.

"He'll find some in the shallows or even up on the beach first," I shouted after them. "Ignore those— they aren't the ones he wants. They just give him an idea where to find the ones he does."

I started the Sea-Doo and pulled the brake all the way, giving the throttle a little bump. When the PWC backed smartly away from the beach, I turned the handlebars. Once perpendicular to shore, I released the brake and gave it a little gas, heading back toward *Ambrosia.*

Savannah was waiting on the work deck, wearing a white bikini with a short beach cover over the top. I slowed and then killed the engine, drifting alongside. She had a boat bag slung over her head and shoulder.

102

"Taxi, Miss?"

Savannah used my shoulders as handrails to climb on behind me. "Did you find them okay?"

"No, I just tossed the boy and the dog on the beach and came back for you."

She smacked my shoulder as I started the Sea-Doo and backed away. Then she put her arms around my waist and pressed herself to my back.

"What did you find out from the ensign?" she asked.

I kept the speed just above an idle. "There's a lot more going on here than just cocaine smuggling, deforestation, and poaching."

"That's a whole lot, right there," Savannah said, resting her chin on my shoulder and watching the water slip past. "What else is there?"

"Jorge and Luna Flores, along with their uncle, Professor Aldrick Mejia, are from a tribe of hunter-gatherers who've lived in the rainforest for thousands of years. They're called the Tawahka and they're facing extinction."

"Extinction?"

"Some Central and South American tribes weren't even discovered until the twentieth century."

"What can we do?" she asked.

We? I thought.

For the most part, Savannah had been content living on *Ambrosia*. She'd been a live-aboard for most of her adult life and nearly all of Flo's. She left the ship to me and the crew, helping when needed, but unless danger got too close, she'd preferred not to involve herself in what *Ambrosia's* mission was.

"Professor Mejia thinks it's too late," I replied. "He doesn't believe there are enough true Tawahka left."

"And the girl was his niece?"

"His sister's daughter," I replied. "Mejia left the tribe as a young boy, not even knowing he had an aunt and uncle. He didn't really expand on that, except to say he'd only learned of his family much later. From what he said, he was very young. He didn't even know he had a niece and nephew until he spoke at her commencement, and she introduced herself."

"The news story I read said she was an ecologist."

"Double PhDs in ecology and evolutionary biology," I said. "She was working on a project that might have helped curtail the extinction of her own people. That makes her loss, being a young woman of pure blood, even more tragic."

"So, I ask again, what can we do?"

"Save the rainforest, I guess," I replied, squeezing the throttle to get the Sea-Doo up on plane.

The truth was, I didn't know what we could do and needed to think about it some more. The sudden acceleration had the desired effect. We'd have to shout to be heard. So, Savannah gripped me tighter, pressing her body to mine.

"Is this as fast as it goes?" she yelled.

"Not quite," I replied.

Suddenly, Savannah stood up, balancing on the back of the machine with her thighs gripping my torso as she leaned forward over my head.

"All ahead full!" she shouted, raising a hand, and pointing in front of us. "Bring me that horizon, Captain!"

"Aye, aye, Commodore!" I shouted back, pulling the throttle lever tight.

CHAPTER FIFTEEN

Carlos Montoya sat on the porch behind the bar. He had a nearly empty beer bottle in his hand as he looked down at the roaring stream. A rain in the Sierra de Agalta mountain range the night before had made the road across the stream, what little of it there was, completely impassible. There was no way to get down to the city.

Being cut off from the civilized world didn't bother Carlos. His place was in the highlands where he was born, and where generations of Pech before him had been born. Twice a week, he made the trek up into the mist. The first half of the journey back to his village was by truck, and then on foot from the village at the end of the rugged road.

He hired men from the village to carry everything. They were known as *la asociaciones*—non-members of the cartel, but men vying to become *oficiales*. Those men carried supplies up to the coca farm and crude lab, then brought pure cocaine back down. It was a two-day round trip, though only eighty-five kilometers.

The coca was grown in a clear-cut area deep in the rainforest, and the drug was manufactured on site. Every month, a new trail was cut through the dense jungle and every few months, a new section was cleared, and a new farm established.

Although most of the government was in the cartel's pocket, there were still a few *policia* who tried to enforce the laws, and it was up to Carlos and a few others to see that they were thwarted.

The midday sun bore down on the bare metal roof over Carlos's head. But the heavy flow in the stream seemed to pull a slight cool breeze along, so sitting in the shade of the porch wasn't overly hot.

"When do you think he will come?" Demian Juarez asked, sitting down adjacent to Carlos, and sliding a fresh beer across the table.

Carlos drained the last from his bottle and sent it flying toward the rocks and water below. It crashed against a boulder with a satisfying sound.

"How long do you think this place will be here?" Carlos asked, ignoring his friend's question.

Demian had asked the same question three times and Carlos had given him the same answer in each case. He didn't know.

"What do you mean?" Demian asked.

"The rain falls in the mountains. The stream floods and washes away more rock and dirt. The edge of the drop-off is only five meters from the steps."

"It has always been five meters away."

"No, it hasn't," Carlos said, pointing to a massive boulder slightly downstream. "Don't you remember? That rock used to be ten meters from these very steps."

"You are worried about being swept away?" Demian asked.

Carlos looked over at his friend and coworker. "That rock was here the day we became *oficiales*."

Demian looked down at the rock in the stream. "Yes, I believe you are—"

"Shut up, you fools!" a voice hissed from out of nowhere.

Both men were quickly on their feet, pulling pistols from under their shirts.

"Who is that?" Carlos shouted.

A figure slowly rose from the edge of the rocks. Carlos had been looking down at the stream and hadn't seen anyone there. He pointed his gun at the man, as did Demian.

"Who are you?" Carlos demanded.

The man was dressed in dark clothing, a long coat hanging from his shoulders. He stepped up out of the gorge as if he were floating.

"Señora Castillo-Cortez said you needed my help."

"El Astilla," Demian breathed softly, as he lowered his gun.

The man moved closer, removing his hat. He looked to be the same age as Carlos and Demian, perhaps a little younger. The three of them were roughly the same height, but El Astilla was broader in the chest and shoulders, and probably heavier than either of the cartel lieutenants by five or ten kilograms.

"You may put down your guns, *señors*," the man said. "I do not have one."

"It is not wise to travel this part of the country unarmed," Carlos said, still unsure of the stranger.

The man stopped at the top of the steps, facing Carlos, just five feet away. His eyes were dark and emotionless. "I said I didn't have a pistol, *amigo*. I did not say I was unarmed."

El Astilla pulled back the sides of his coat to reveal the shiny black hilts on custom-made machetes hung on either hip.

"Now put away your pistol and tell me about this *indígena* before I cut off your fucking hand."

CHAPTER SIXTEEN

I killed the engine as we idled toward the beach, and when the Sea-Doo's hull brushed the sand, Savannah stepped off. I got off and pulled the machine up as high on the beach as I could.

The tide was rising, so I opened the compartment and took out one of the sand augers Antonio had shown me, along with a ten-foot dock line that had loops on either end.

Each loop had an aluminum carabiner clipped to it and I clicked one onto the tow hook on the front of the PWC, then tossed the other end up on the sand.

Twisting the T-handled auger, I screwed it into the sand, then realized there was nothing on it to clip the other carabiner to. On the side near the top was a threaded hole, which I assumed was where another part would be screwed into, to hold a beach umbrella in place. I removed the carabiner and stuffed the loop through the hole and pulled it out of the top. When I clipped the carabiner back on, it was too big to fit through the hole, so it held the line in place.

"Pretty ingenious," Savannah said, watching me.

"Antonio came up with it," I said, giving the line a test tug. It held fast, even with me pulling harder on it than the Sea-Doo might in a strong current. "Probably better than having a steel anchor banging around in the storage box."

"Where're Ross and Kassandra?" Savannah asked, looking around.

"They were farther down the beach," I replied, taking her boat bag, and leading the way in the opposite direction. "We'll go this way and wade around the lagoon to see if we can find any mussels."

"How'd you know that was where I'd seen them?"

"I didn't," I replied. "Mussels are more abundant in cooler waters up north. But they can sometimes be found in intertidal zones in the tropics."

"How do we know which kind are edible?"

"I have no idea," I admitted. "But Marcos will know."

We crossed the tip of the sandbar into Turtle Lagoon, then followed the mangroves lining the shore.

"Over there's where I saw a whole bunch of them," Savannah said, pointing toward an area of seagrass. "All through there, in the shallows."

I took her hand and we waded through knee-deep water, shuffling our feet across the bottom.

Stingrays loved lagoons like the one we were in and if you stepped on one, their natural reaction would be to skewer your calf or ankle with their barb. Nudge one in the side and it was more likely to just swim quickly away.

"Are you doing okay with life on *Ambrosia*?" I asked.

"You asked me that same question just the other day."

"I mean with what we're doing," I said. "Not actually living aboard the boat. I know you like that."

"What's not to like?" she said with a laugh. "It's the most luxurious boat I've ever been on. But I feel bad for the crew sometimes."

"How so?"

110

"Our quarters are pretty opulent, Jesse. Two bedrooms, two heads, a private galley and patio? Meanwhile, the rest of the crew live in an eight- by-eight box crammed two to a room."

"Has anyone complained?" I asked.

"Of course not," she replied. "It's just kind of like eating ice cream in front of a starving dog."

"You're dodging the question."

"You know I support you in whatever you do," she said. "I understand the danger. I wish it didn't exist, but it does. There will always be people who do bad things. Fortunately, there are people like you to stand in their way."

"And you're okay with that?"

"Well, you're no spring chicken," she said, splashing water on me. "So, don't push it, okay?"

I bent and plucked a mussel from a small rock, its threads stretching before letting go. "Are these the ones you were talking about?"

"That one's kind of puny," she replied, then pointed a little farther along the shoreline. "There are bigger ones clustered in the seagrass."

She took the bag from me and reached inside. "We can put them in this spare tote bag."

"Boat bag," I said. "If it's on a boat, it's a boat bag."

She picked up a much larger mussel than the one I had and dropped it into the spare bag. "We're not on the boat," she said.

I had no idea what kind of mussels they were, but there were plenty of them. We filled the bag in no time at all, then headed back to where we'd left the Sea-Doo.

"Flo called this morning," Savannah said, as we walked back across the spit of sand separating the lagoon from the bay.

111

"Is something wrong?"

"No, she just called to talk. David got back okay and they're getting a place together."

David Stone, our daughter's fiancé, had been working aboard *Ambrosia* for the last several months, foregoing a semester at University of Florida, where they both attended. He'd flown back to Florida a week earlier.

"How do you feel about that?" I asked.

"It doesn't matter what I think," she replied. "She's an adult now."

The tide had risen slightly and the PWC was nearly floating again. I opened the storage compartment and took the second dock line out, quickly tying the bag to the handlebar, so it dangled in the water.

"Yeah, they're both adults," I agreed, "and they're engaged, but that doesn't mean you can't have an opinion on their living together."

"Oh, please, Jesse. You and I lived together for over a year before we got married."

She had a point there. But we were older. I decided not to press the point. "Want to hang out here on the beach for a while?"

"Does Ross have his phone with him?"

"I think so," I replied. "I'll call him and tell him where we are. I might have to make three runs to get us back to the boat."

I pulled up Ross's number and called.

"I was just about to call you," he said in his Oklahoma drawl. "Your dog's amazing. We already have about four dozen clams."

"Is Alberto behaving?"

"He's almost as good as Finn at digging them up," Ross replied. "Yeah, he's being a perfect little man."

We've got a bag full of mussels," I told him. "We're on the east side of Turtle Lagoon, near that long sandbar."

"We're only about a quarter mile away," he said. "Want us to meet you there?"

I looked over at Savannah. She already had a blanket spread out on the sand and was pulling her beach cover off over her head, shaking her hair loose.

"Yeah," I said into the phone, watching her. "We're going to relax on the sand for a bit."

"Roger that," Ross said. "We'll be there in about half an hour, probably."

Savannah stretched her long, tan legs luxuriously on the blanket.

"Take your time," I told Ross. "We're in no hurry."

CHAPTER SEVENTEEN

After getting everyone back to *Ambrosia*, Ross and I carried the bags of shellfish down to the galley, where Marcos and Grady made room on a countertop, then dumped them all out.

"*Perfecto*," Marcos said, picking up two of the mussels. "*Mejillón azul*, the blue mussel."

"They're edible?" I asked.

"*Si, Capitán.* Very good."

"They don't get any better," Grady added. "And they're found just about everywhere." He paused and picked up one of the clams. "But these are the prize. Where'd you find clams around here?"

"The captain's dog found them," Ross said. "He actually dove and dug them up from the bottom in about four or five feet of water. Once he showed me where to dig, we got a bunch in short order."

"Your *dog?*" Grady asked me.

"Ever since he was a pup," I replied. "Some dogs like jerky treats. Finn likes clams."

"If the divers get the conchs," Marcos said, separating the shellfish into buckets, "we will have all we need to prepare the meal."

"Great," I told him. "Does Matt have any idea what's going on?"

"I do not think so," Marcos replied.

Grady laughed. "Val has been keeping him occupied."

"I'm almost afraid to ask how."

"They took the other Sea-Doo," Grady explained, "And went around to the other side of the island for lunch. Whenever they're aboard, she keeps his nose in a book."

"He's studying for his captain's license," I said.

I left the two chefs to their tasks and went up to my quarters to clean up. Savannah's bikini and Alberto's shorts were hanging outside on the towel rack, but neither of them was there. Nor was Finn. On a ship as big as *Ambrosia*, there was a lot to do. But what I needed to do first was get a shower. I was almost crusty from salt and sand.

Water wasn't an issue on board with *Ambrosia's* reverse osmosis system. The water maker could supply enough fresh drinking water for a small village if called upon.

So, I took a longer shower than normal, getting the salt out of my hair and the rest of the sand off my body.

The drains from all the showers on *Ambrosia* flowed right back to the sea. As much time as Savannah and I were spending rolling around in the sand lately, I envisioned a new sandbar forming below the hull.

Feeling human again and wearing clean clothes, I went up to the bridge deck, just to check on the ship's status. Axel was on duty and Crystal was keeping him company.

Jack Armstrong didn't have any rules about male and female crew fraternization. He'd told me that he made sure anyone hired was a responsible adult who could either accept the possible fallout after becoming involved with a shipmate or could transfer to another job.

Savannah and I weren't the only couple on board. There were two other married couples—Marcos and Mayra, and their eldest daughter Giselle and her husband, Ricardo. And it appeared a few other romances were forming.

"How'd the mussel and clam hunt go?" Axel asked, his Mississippi accent dripping with magnolia nectar.

"Got enough of both," I replied, glancing back into the empty operations center. "Anything going on?"

"Not much," he replied. "A sailboat passed about thirty minutes ago, but I haven't seen any other water traffic. Roger was up here looking for you a few minutes ago."

Just then, Roger Tanaka came in the port hatch, grinned, and pointed at me. "I found him," he said to Axel, who chuckled.

"What's up?" I asked Roger.

"It'd be easier to show you," Roger said, leading the way back to his station. He tapped a key to wake up his monitor, entered his pass code, then stepped back so I could see the screen.

There was a news story in Spanish, but I got the gist of it. There had been a number of jaguar attacks on people in mainland Honduras recently.

"Jaguar attacks?" I asked Roger.

"This line here," Roger said, pointing toward the second paragraph from the bottom. "It says three of the five victims belonged to the Chóloma cartel. And the other two were known associates of theirs."

I reread what I could understand. "It says the attacks all occurred in and around the Río Plátano Biosphere Reserve. Or am I not getting it right?"

"That is correct," Crystal said, looking over my shoulder. "And the cartel leader thinks the killings were intentional."

"Intentional?" I asked. "Sorry. My Spanish isn't nearly as good as your English. Does it say how he thought it was intentional? Does he

117

mean someone had trained or was controlling the jaguars?"

"The Cholóma cartel *capo* isn't a man," Roger said. "It's a woman named Paloma Castillo-Cortez."

"Cholóma is a long way from the Río Plátano," I said.

"Over two hundred miles," Roger agreed, nodding. "And much of it on rocky roads or even on foot. But the cartels use the remoteness of the interior's rainforests to their advantage."

"I'll accept that," I said. "But how do wild animal attacks tie in with the murders of Luna Flores and the others?"

"Many of the murders took place in the small towns and villages that border the biosphere," Roger said. "The fact that Miss Flores was killed in La Ceiba doesn't mean much."

"How so?"

He straightened and looked up at me. "She'd just returned to La Ceiba after conducting a biological survey in a remote part of the reserve."

"What did you find out about the cartel leader?"

Using the mouse, Roger brought up another news article with the headline, *Nueva escuela abre en* Cholóma —New school opens in Cholóma .

Below the headline was a picture of four people—three men and a woman. The men were dressed in suits and the woman in a black skirt, matching jacket, and white blouse, with a pale green scarf around her neck. She was exceptionally beautiful.

"Paloma Castillo-Cortez is a hero to the people in the Sula Valley," Roger said. "This is the second school the cartel has built in as many years. Her late husband, Pablo Castillo-Cortez, was the head of the operation until he was killed by a rival in San Pedro Sula."

"I thought it was common in Hispanic culture for a married

woman to keep her own name," I remarked, then glanced at Crystal. "But your sister didn't adhere to that, either."

"It is common, yes," Crystal replied. "My sister *chose* to take her husband's name. I would suspect Paloma Castillo-Cortez took her husband's name, a combination of his paternal and maternal surnames, to maintain some legitimacy within the cartel."

Roger nodded. "Before her late husband controlled the Cholóma cartel, his father, Juan Castillo ran it, until he died. The elder Castillo had arranged the marriage of Pablo to Paloma. Less than a week after Pablo's death, the rival who'd killed him, along with his entire family were slaughtered—his and his wife's parents, their kids, even a granddaughter. The rival was the last to die. It seemed the elder Castillo knew that his chosen daughter-in-law was far more ruthless than his son ever was."

"And she thinks her cartel soldiers were killed by someone with trained jaguars?" I asked. "The idea's ridiculous."

"I'm sure it is," Roger agreed. "But it doesn't matter, Captain. She controls a lot of very dangerous people. Men who would stop at nothing to wipe out every great cat in the country if she told them to."

"The plot just keeps getting thicker," I said. "Anything else on the Metis from anyone?"

"No," Roger replied. "But Mr. Armstrong assigned two analysts to the case."

The satellite phone in the bridge chimed and Axel hurried to answer it. He listened for a moment and then replied, "Right away, sir."

"That was Mr. Armstrong, himself," Axel said, returning to Roger's station. "He said you should follow your instincts and see what can be done about the activist's murders."

The link was tenuous. I knew that. My old friend and business partner, Deuce Livingston, would say it was a long reach to connect the two events. But the cartel leader was the one doing the connecting. If she was responsible for ordering the assassinations and thought someone was seeking revenge against her organization, her history of dealing with rivals dictated she would seek swift retribution.

I paced the deck between the op center and the bridge, thinking. If she wanted to, she could easily order her people to hunt down and kill every jaguar in the area, just as Roger had said. The common denominator between the murders and the jaguar attacks, whether the cats were trained or just hungry, was Paloma Castillo-Cortez.

Louis Pasteur once said that chance favored the prepared mind. I'd tried to keep my wits at the ready for whenever Lady Luck showed her face, and by doing so, things often just fell right into my lap.

Ambrosia was in the Bay Islands by chance. My only connection to anything going on with the cartel, the conservationists, the rainforest, or for that matter, even the jaguars, was that I happened to be there, and a Honduran naval officer had confided in me about his dead sister.

Jorge and Luna Flores, along with their uncle, Aldrick Mejia, were the ties that brought me and Armstrong Research into the picture.

I made my decision. "Axel, organize a research party to include yourself, me, Ross, Duster, and Gerald. Have them pack for an overnighter, maybe two. Call the dive boats back and get Matt and Val back here. *Ambrosia* is going to La Ceiba."

CHAPTER EIGHTEEN

It had only taken an hour to get underway. Matt and Val had been headed back when Axel called them, as was one of the tenders. So, we only needed to wait for the second boat. They'd been diving a reef just a few miles away.

"What's going on?" Savannah asked, coming onto the bridge with Alberto and Fernando.

"We're preparing to get underway," I replied. "Jack gave me the green light to find out what we can and do something to stop it."

"Is there anything I can do to help?"

"We're going to La Ceiba," I said. "Then I'm taking a group of men into the jungle."

"What?" she asked with alarm. "You can't—"

"I can and I will," I told her with resolve. "Look, babe, I was put here for a reason. Why? I have no idea. But I'm good at what I do and only get better with age."

She started to protest; I could see the fire in her eyes. Just as quickly, it went away. "Then you should restrict everyone to the ship, so you have nothing to worry about. And I'll take part in the watch."

I grinned. "I would have thought of that."

When Val and Matt arrived, I made an excuse and left him in charge on the bridge while I went down to help Antonio get the boats stowed in the garage. The divers had found a few conchs, which Kris Carter took down to the galley.

Although we had a job to do, I wasn't forgetting Matt's birthday and had every intention of being back to the dock before his dinner. My old platoon sergeant, Deuce's father, Russ Livingston, always said that if an objective couldn't be taken in a single day, you should back off and flank the enemy, then attack from a different direction.

Though the distance was less than thirty miles, I had Axel keep *Ambrosia* at trawler speed. The water between the Bay Islands and the mainland was a busy sea lane for cruising divers.

Besides, I knew preparations would likely have to be made for such a large boat at the ferry terminal, really the only dock big enough, and anchoring offshore could be choppy, with wave action from the east and the outflow from the Cangrejal River from the south. I called the ferry terminal as soon as we were underway.

La Ceiba is primarily known as the gateway to the Bay Islands and Galaxy Wave ran a regular schedule to Roatan twice a day, departing La Ceiba mid-morning and late afternoon.

When I told the dockmaster we were a research vessel and how big *Ambrosia* was, he informed me that they could make room for us, but it would take a couple of hours.

I glanced down at the chart plotter as Axel started turning the ship wide around the east end of Utila. "It will take us about that long to get there," I told the man over the ship's satellite phone. "We're just leaving Utila."

"Hail on VHF 68 when you are near the mouth of the harbor, Captain," he said. "The ship channel is clearly marked and recently dredged. If you arrive before we are ready, you will not be able to anchor inside the harbor. Sorry—regulations."

"We won't," I replied.

We wouldn't need to. *Ambrosia's* station-keeping system would keep the bow and stern in a fixed position indefinitely.

"Will you be requiring fuel or anything else?" the dockmaster asked.

Marinas made good money on dock space. For a boat of *Ambrosia's* size, a single night at a dock in most places would run well over a thousand dollars and twice that in bigger tourist-cruising destinations. But fuel was where they made the big markup, sometimes double what they paid for it.

"We're fully provisioned," I told the man, "but I like to top off the tanks whenever we stop. We'll need close to two thousand gallons."

I could hear cash register noises coming out of the man's ears. I thanked him and hung up the phone.

"Wasson, Cap'n?" Matt asked. "That was a right proper anchorage we left. Are we back on the bleddy clock?"

"It looks that way," I replied. "I'm going to take a group ashore to see what we can find out about the murders of those activists. There've been some developments." I handed Matt the secondary bridge Metis, opened to the file Roger had created. "You and Val get caught up and let me know your thoughts in a couple of hours. Feel free to add any comments to Roger's notes you think might be important."

"Aye, Cap'n," he said, taking it and nodding toward the port hatch for Val to follow him.

They left the bridge, I assumed headed down to the cockpit or one of their cabins, but a moment later I saw them making their way onto the foredeck, sitting on the big sun pad.

The side hatch opened, and Gerald Montague entered. "Good afternoon, Captain," he said, nodding toward a corner. I followed

123

him and he spoke in a low voice. "Are we to be armed on this 'research' party?"

Gerald was a retired former spec-ops soldier, and with Travis Stockwell back in Bimini running the security team there, Gerald was second-in-command of *Ambrosia's* security team. His boss was Jeff Oswald, a former command sergeant major with the 101st Airborne Division, where the two men had served together.

"Very covertly," I replied. "We'll be posing as geologists, making a quick foray into the mountains."

"You said pack for a night or two," he said. "A geological survey could take months."

Gerald was a retired master sergeant in his late forties, black, several inches shorter than me, and very athletic. He was also bilingual, speaking fluent Spanish.

"Only a handful of people will ask what we're doing and I'm counting on them not knowing anything about it and not asking anything more."

"And geologists usually work with local guides."

I arched an eyebrow. "How do you know all this?"

"Whenever I took leave from the Army, I spent a lot of time as an amateur prospector. Did it full time after leaving the service, and before Jeff contacted me about this gig."

"Is that right?" I asked. "Ever find anything?"

"I found enough that my kids will never have to work a day in their lives, no matter how crazy I get with their inheritance," he replied. Then he looked around at the others on the bridge. "More than half the crew here was chosen based on the same criteria the field operatives were."

Years ago, when Charity had first contacted me about working for Armstrong Research, she'd told me that one of the things they

124

insisted on for their operatives was that they be independently wealthy. Jack didn't like quibbling over pay and didn't want anyone who put financial gain ahead of the mission.

"I know of someone who'd make a good guide," I told him. "If he's available."

"Who?" Gerald asked.

"A man from a nearly extinct local tribe."

"Does he speak any English?"

I nodded and grinned. "He's a professor at Harvard University."

"How does a primitive culture produce a Harvard professor?"

"He was orphaned in the jungle as a boy," I replied. "A Peace Corps volunteer found him and took him in, raised him and gave him an education. Humans are capable of learning anything. Primitive cultures just never needed to. I'll see if I can reach him."

After finding Jorge's number in my contacts, I called him. He answered on the first ring. "I am told you are leaving."

"Leaving?" I asked, wondering how he'd learned so quickly that we'd weighed anchor. "No, we're on our way to La Ceiba. I want to go into the biosphere, but we need transportation and a guide. Do you think your uncle would be available?"

There was a rustling sound, then muffled voices. After a moment, Jorge said, "Where are you coming to?"

"The ferry dock in three hours," I replied.

"We will be there."

"We?" I asked.

"I have resigned from the navy," he said. "I cannot work for a government that allows these things to go on."

CHAPTER NINETEEN

Gustavo Ramos squatted behind the giant buttress roots of an ancient ceiba tree, studying the ground. To an untrained eye, the forest floor looked like a random scattering of leaves and twigs. It was wet and covered with the detritus of centuries—fallen branches on top of leaves, covered by giant rotting tree trunks, one after another after another for thousands of years, the broken-down remains piling on top of each other.

But Gustavo could see alterations to the chaotic mess. He could tell that someone had once hidden between the giant roots. He'd remained for some time, moving very little. A broken leaf, a crumb of food, the slight odor of urine.

"You said you searched for the body," Gustavo said to the two men with him. "Did you also search for the man?"

"We found no sign of anyone," Carlos replied. "What was left of the body was found two kilometers away."

"The belly was ripped open and the cat ate his organs," Gustavo said, waving a hand in frustration. "Yes, yes, you told me that. It is what they do. But you didn't say anything about the man who hid here waiting for our *soldados*."

"We looked everywhere," Demian said, peering down into the narrow space between the massive roots.

Gustavo stepped back, giving them both a better look. "A man was hiding right here," he said. "The sign is faint, but there."

"Then it is true," Carlos said, his voice a sigh. "*El hombre gato.*"

"A cat man?" Gustavo asked in a mocking tone. "Was it a man's head on a cat's body, or a cat's head on a man's?"

Carlos looked at him with fire in his eyes. "We are not simple children, afraid of the dark. It is a man who controls the cats somehow."

"Look around, fool," Gustavo said, pushing the man. "Do you see any tracks here from a jaguar? No, this man does not control the great cats. I think he summons them somehow."

"My apologies, El Astilla," Carlos said. "Can you see where the man went?"

Gustavo, known by very few as "The Sliver," professed to being able to track an iguana across a rock. But whoever had hidden among the giant buttress roots had left very little sign of his presence.

"Not with all the tracks your people made," he said. "But I have a feeling he will come back to this place."

Demian looked around nervously. "What should we do?"

"He won't return if we are here," Gustavo said. "Whoever this man is, he is good at hiding his tracks. I think you are right that he is one of the *indígena*. What is that village where we left the truck?"

It does not have a name," Carlos said. "The people are Tawahka, a backwards bunch of monkeys unable to learn anything."

"There will be hunters among them," Gustavo said. "Perhaps we can enlist a few to help find this '*hombre gato*' you speak of."

"They will be of no help," Demian said. "They have been pacified for many years and rely on the government now to survive."

"Do they understand money?"

"*Sí*, El Astilla," Carlos said. "We hire them as carriers for a few lempira. They use it to buy tobacco."

"I will offer a thousand lempira to any man among them who can track this man."

It was probably more money than any of the natives had ever seen, though it was barely forty American dollars.

"If we hurry, we can be back here before sunset," Carlos said.

"I will wait here," Gustavo said. "Bring at least one man who knows the forest better than you two."

"You will stay here?" Demian asked. "Alone?"

Gustavo turned and looked down at the trail. "We are *all* alone, *amigos*. We are born alone and we die alone. It is what I prefer."

"We will return as quickly as possible," Carlos offered.

The two men left, moving along the trail. It was a new trail, only a few weeks old, but the jungle was relentless and was already trying to remove any sign that man had been there.

Gustavo went down to the trail after they'd left. Finding the spot of the attack was easy. There was dried blood all over, turned black by the heat, as well as white powder scattered around. Where the two came in contact, the crusty mixture was brownish pink.

Thick, dried blood drops clung to the trunks of nearby trees. The great cat must have gotten to the man's neck, spraying the leaves and trees with his life force.

As he turned, a glimmer of reflected light caught Gustavo's eye. Very little sunlight filtered down to the ground in the rainforest and the jungle floor was covered by leaves, rotting deadfalls, branches, and a few moss-covered rocks—nothing that would reflect light.

When he tried to find the spot again, he couldn't—the shaft of light had disappeared. But he knew he'd seen something there. Gustavo moved back along the trail toward where he'd spotted the faint reflection, eyes searching the ground.

"There," he whispered, stopping in his tracks.

He squatted and examined what appeared to be a tiny shard of glass on a large stone. Looking closer, he could see smaller flecks of something around it.

After putting a finger to the spot, he raised it to his nose, and the putrid scent nearly caused him to gag.

"*Qué demonios?*" he muttered, wiping his finger on his pant leg.

CHAPTER TWENTY

Jorge and Aldrick were waiting at the ferry dock when we tied up to the quay. I kissed Savannah and rustled Alberto's hair. Then, leaving Matt in charge of the fueling operation, I went down to the cockpit with Ross and Axel. Gerald and Duster were already there.

The five of us were dressed similarly—nondescript, heavy work clothes and boots.

"Everyone armed?" I asked, before we started down to the work platform.

All nodded and I led the way, introducing my "research team" to the former Honduran Naval officer and his uncle.

"We will go to my village," Aldrick said. "There may be some there who know more of what is going on in the forest."

"We have machetes in the truck," Jorge said. "In case you want to go farther into the jungle."

The truck was a small Kia flatbed with dual wheels in the back. The bed had a bench seat on either side. It was a cab over, which gave it a short wheelbase, and I could tell by the locking front hubs that it was six- wheel drive.

"Do not let the size fool you, Captain," Jorge said, as we walked toward the truck. "The Bongo is a stout little truck as long as it is not overloaded."

"What's that?" Duster asked. "Five hundred pounds?"

Jorge glanced over at the man. "Over one thousand kilos."

"We'll ride in back," I said. "And remember, we're geologists. Calling me Captain will give us away."

"There is room for three in front," Aldrick said, moving toward the passenger side.

"Go ahead," Axel said. "What should we call you?"

I looked questioningly toward Gerald.

"Doctor or professor, probably," he said.

"Dr. McDermitt," I said, grinning. "Mam and Pap would have been so proud."

I followed Aldrick around to the passenger side and climbed in behind him. He slid open the back window and turned, speaking to the men in back. "There is water in the cooler. The journey will take two hours, but we will rarely go over fifty kilometers per hour."

"You have no accent," Gerald said, sitting next to the opening in the glass.

"I'm a nutmegger," Aldrick said with a New England accent. "I tone it down, when possible, but I was raised in Connecticut."

"But you're from a small tribe in the jungle? I'm curious about that, Professor."

"Curiosity is a good thing," Aldrick said. "It needs constant feeding. Please, just all me Aldrick."

"You're a for-real professor at Harvard?" Gerald asked. "Not an honorary title or anything?"

Aldrick nodded, as Jorge started driving through La Ceiba. "I was offered an academic scholarship when I was sixteen," he said. "I graduated from University of Connecticut at nineteen, with a BS in biology. Then I was offered a chance to go to Yale for my PhD." He shrugged. "Yale offered me a job when I finished, but Harvard offered more. At the time, I was career-focused."

"You don't look like a professor," Duster said, sitting across from Gerald.

"I shall take that as a compliment," he said. "As I've gotten older, my focus has been more and more on my people and other indigenous tribes."

"Excuse me for saying this," Gerald began.

I was ready for just about anything, considering the man's frank openness and curiosity.

"I assumed people who lived in the jungle lacked the intellect to survive in the modern world, and that was why they remained hidden."

"The reason most tribes avoided modern society has little to do with intellect," Aldrick countered. "Early in colonial history, contact with outsiders brought death, either by the sword or by disease. Many of those who survived first contact were enslaved."

"So, what kept these tribes from evolving?"

"You mean like Europeans?"

Gerald nodded.

"When humans first moved out of Africa, they spread across Southern Europe and Asia at first. Today, many of the native people of what most would consider 'backward' cultures live near the equator—the rainforests of Amazonia, the native tribes of the southern United States and Mexico, the Polynesian islands, and Southeast Asia. They didn't have to adapt the way Europeans did."

"How so?" Axel asked, now listening intently.

"As humans migrated northward through Europe and Asia," Aldrick began, "they encountered many hardships, the greatest of all being the climate. Cold weather meant clothing, and clothing

133

meant skinning animals, which required more advanced tools. The farther we, as a species, migrated away from the equator, the higher the need for adaptation. My people evolved much the same as yours, but we didn't have to adapt to a harsh environment."

The miles slowly rolled by as we passed from the city to the countryside. Then we started up into the mountains, where the pavement turned to dirt and finally, rocks. The truck proved to be exactly what was needed on the rough road.

The jungle started closing in, and even though it was still a couple of hours before sunset, it grew darker. I looked up at the canopy, high above. Colorful birds flew from branch to branch.

Finally, Jorge had to stop and lock the front axles as the road turned to mud and slippery rocks. So, everyone climbed out to stretch their legs for a few minutes.

The humidity was probably close to one hundred percent, which was why they were called rainforests. Even if rain wasn't falling from the sky, moisture in the air condensed on everything, leaving the jungle looking like it had just received a passing shower.

"We are in the Río Plátano Biosphere now," Aldrick said. "I haven't been here in ten years."

"Why?" I asked.

"A very good question, my friend. For the last decade, I've traveled the world on behalf of all aboriginal people, speaking before councils and hearings, explaining that even though ethnic groups like mine and countless others live a lifestyle that outsiders might think primitive, we are, in fact, just as evolved. I even spoke to the United Nations General Assembly once."

"Target fixation," Gerald said, as we all climbed back into the little flatbed truck. "That's what fighter pilots call it, when they're so focused on chasing after one plane, they miss two more coming up their tailpipe."

Aldrick looked back through the window over his shoulder and smiled. "A very apropos description. My focus then was very narrow."

Jorge climbed back in, and we bounced along for another forty minutes as he drove steadily up through the mist.

The wipers and headlights came on and the road got rougher as the dense jungle seemed to crowd in around us. Eventually, we topped a hill, where Jorge stopped at a spot overlooking a small village.

It was more of an oval-shaped clearing, with a stream running through the middle of it. There were dozens of primitive structures, raised a few feet off the ground and built out of materials from the forest. I counted thirty-one. Each of them faced the stream and a central area, where a thin curl of smoke rose from two cook fires.

An older Toyota 4x4 was parked at the north end of the village, where a road, presumably the one we were on, came out of the forest and dead-ended at the stream.

"Is the truck being here unusual?" I asked.

"No," Jorge replied. "Luna told me a truck comes up here twice a week with supplies for the coca farm and the lab where they make the cocaine, then carries the drug into the city."

"In an open flatbed?" Duster asked, a look of incredulousness on his face. "If you know where it is, why don't the police go in and bust them?"

"Most of the police and many government officials in this country are corrupt," Jorge replied. "We rely heavily on tourism money coming into the Bay Islands, so there, and in La Ceiba, for the most part, there is far less crime. But on the mainland, and especially out here in the jungle... Well, the laws don't reach out here. The police line their pockets with blood money and turn a blind eye on the people."

"We will leave the truck here and go down on foot," Aldrick said. "It will only take an hour and if they leave, we will hear them. But it is many hours to the farm and back."

Gerald started to say something from the rear window, but I silenced him with a look.

If Aldrick hadn't been here in ten years, I thought, *how would he know how far away the farm was located?*

Jorge found a spot and parked the truck behind a massive deadfall covered in vines. The vines draping the ancient branches hid the truck from the road completely. Then Aldrick led the way across the road and into the rainforest.

I thought about asking Aldrick about the farm's location. Maybe there was only one place up there that was close enough and suitable for planting. It could be that the villagers had used it in the past to grow crops. But I decided that for now, I'd just wait.

Though I'd already checked and rechecked it, I pulled my Sig from under my jacket and press-checked the slide just enough to see the copper jacket of a 9mm round in the chamber. With what was in the magazine, the sound of eighteen rapid shots would likely scare some people to death. And there were five of us, similarly armed. Maybe six—I couldn't tell if Jorge was carrying.

Whoever was driving the Toyota we'd seen wouldn't be so easily frightened. Violent death was a way of life among many drug cartels. If I had to, I'd shoot to kill, not frighten.

We moved quietly down a trail that seemed well traveled. I followed behind Aldrick. The man's feet made no sound as he led us down the mountainside. Behind me, his nephew wasn't nearly so quiet, but in the thick forest, his occasional misstep, or the snap of a twig likely wasn't heard more than twenty feet away.

Other than Jorge, I heard nothing behind me. I and my crew were very adept at moving silently, and we were no strangers to walking; we'd all once been infantrymen. Nor were we unfamiliar with walking in hostile territory. I knew that like me, they were looking and listening. They wouldn't be bunched up. There wasn't any need to talk.

A little less than halfway down, Aldrick stopped and stood still.

I stepped up beside him on the left. "What is it?" I whispered, not seeing anything.

"We are not alone," he whispered back, his eyes fixed on a spot just ahead.

Instinctively, I reached for my sidearm, but Aldrick put a hand on mine. "Wait."

I'd been in jungles before. When I'd first enlisted, the country was only six years out of Vietnam and most of the NCOs I trained under had spent time in the jungles there. We trained in similar environments, but in that Honduran rainforest, I felt a bit overwhelmed. Life in this part of the world hadn't changed in thousands of years, maybe tens of thousands.

A full minute slowly ticked past, then another, as we stood silently waiting. The passage of time had no meaning in the rainforest. It was there and had always been there. The deadfall we'd parked the truck behind could have been a tall tree before the time of Christ, reaching for the canopy high overhead. It may have sprouted from the soil before recorded time.

I was on full alert, my senses heightened. I could hear sounds all around us—birds flitting from tree to tree, stopping occasionally to emit strange, repetitive calls. In the distance, a howler monkey called out. Even the sound of water dripping onto the soft, leafy ground reached my ears. But I heard nothing unusual, nothing out of place or threatening.

Just the forest.

Where Aldrick was staring, I saw nothing but jungle. All around us, only the trail itself gave any visual indication that humans were within a thousand miles of where we stood.

Or perhaps a thousand years.

It was like being transported through time, back to the dawn of creation, where nothing but the primordial forest existed—deep, dark places, where little light reached the ground and colors faded to shades of gray and black.

Suddenly, a man appeared just ten feet in front of us. It was almost as if he'd materialized out of the mist. He wore tattered gray pants and a gray plaid shirt that had also seen better days. With his dark skin and graying hair, the blotchy pattern of gray was perfect camouflage in the mist. He looked old, with lines etched deeply in his face, though I had no idea what old meant in this place. A primitive life in the jungle could be short and the man might be only forty.

He shouted something in a language I'd never heard. Aldrick took a step forward and replied to the man in what I assumed was the Tawahka language.

I could sense others watching us. This man wasn't alone in the jungle. Others were hiding in the mist, behind great leaves dripping with condensation.

Being a former Marine Corps scout/sniper, I knew where *I'd* be if I were on the opposing side. My eyes fixed on the roots of a large tree. Not prop roots like a mangrove, but tall, thick roots that spread for dozens of feet across the ground, growing upward several feet to create thick, winding walls where a man could easily take cover and conceal himself.

That was where I'd make my hide.

Slowly, a second man rose from the roots I was staring at. Though I hadn't seen or heard him, I knew he was there. Had he sensed that he'd been spotted?

He looked much like the man in front of us, graying hair, lined face, and tattered clothes. He lifted a leg and stepped over the root he'd been hiding behind, saying something to Aldrick.

The professor turned to look at the second man. In his profile, I saw the flicker of recognition when the man spoke.

Aldrick moved toward the newcomer, who advanced steadily until they embraced in a way that only family members would do.

The man stepped back and called out. Three other men, younger than the first two, rose and came out of the mist. Five men, dressed mostly in tatters, carrying bows and long blow guns. One had an antique bolt-action rifle.

A hunting party.

Aldrick turned and faced the rest of us. "It is okay," he said. "Jorge, come and meet another uncle."

CHAPTER TWENTY-ONE

The family reunion was short-lived. The hunting party was led by a man named Ignacio Mejia, Aldrick's older brother. None of the Tawahka men spoke English, and only Ignacio and the other older man spoke their native language, so they switched to Spanish, talking excitedly.

Gerald translated what he could, and what was important. The hunting party was apparently on their way back to the village after two days in the jungle. But when they'd seen the truck in the village, they decided to wait until the cartel soldiers left, even if it meant staying put overnight.

When they'd heard our truck stop, they set up an ambush, thinking we might be a rival of the cartel and there to cause trouble. In the jungle, the enemy of your enemy wasn't always a friend.

I looked around.

"They picked a good pinch point," Duster said, also scanning the area. "I was just getting a jittery feeling when the professor stopped."

"He's telling them about the girl's death," Gerald said, then recounted all that he could keep up with.

The five villagers clustered around Jorge and his uncle had at first been overjoyed by the news of family members outside the forest but were immediately saddened that Ignacio's unknown niece had been murdered in the streets of La Ceiba. Ignacio fell to his knees and sobbed openly for a niece he never met. In a moment of comradeship few ever experienced, the other members of the hunting party lifted Ignacio to his feet, and they all huddled together, embracing, sobbing, and comforting not just the girl's brother and uncles, but each other. They knew what the loss of just one of their own young people meant.

The display touched me. It stirred all of us. I had no idea if what we were witnessing had meaning in their culture, but it did in ours. We'd all experienced the pain of losing a comrade, but the anguish had often been pushed aside to finish the mission. It was further suppressed during the rigid and structured battlefield funeral, with only the fallen comrade's rifle and boots in attendance. Many in the formation might shed a tear while at the position of attention but then, when the order was given to fall out, grown men—warriors— would melt in tears, huddling with their buddies in grief.

The group broke up and the hunters picked up bundles they'd hidden, wrapped in banana leaves and twine made from vines. I assumed it was the wild game they'd hunted.

Aldrick and Jorge returned to our group as the hunters disappeared into the mist, heading down the mountain.

"I will go with them into the village," Aldrick said. "They will leave their catch at the edge of the clearing for you to watch over, while we go in to see if the cartel people are there, or if they are still up in the mountains."

"Aren't we already up in the mountains?" Ross asked.

"The range on the far side of the valley is higher," Aldrick explained. "That is where they have clear-cut areas of the forest to grow the coca."

"Why would they leave their catch?" Duster asked.

Aldrick looked past me to the younger man. "When the cartel people leave, they often take whatever they want. The people of the village leave the government food where it is more easily found, having recently returned to the traditional way of finding food—in the forest."

We started down the mountain again, Aldrick following behind his brother's group. At the edge of the forest, the hunters stopped and dropped their leaf-wrapped bundles next to a log.

"Wait here," Aldrick said.

Jorge started to move along with Aldrick, but he stopped him. "You look too out of place. Wait here with the others."

We all got small, with Duster and Axel on either flank and Gerald watching our six.

"When was the last time you were here?" Ross whispered to Jorge.

"Last week," he replied, a sad expression on his face. "To pick up Luna. I didn't know Ignacio lived here and he was on a hunting trip. Before that, not since I was a small boy. Luna was born here. I was born in La Ceiba. Our parents stopped bringing me here when Luna went off to college. When she returned, she came here often and told me about our people." He paused, then added, "I was too busy to listen."

"You might have other family here," Ross said. "Other aunts and uncles, probably cousins, too."

"Aldrick's family was almost all killed," Jorge said. "His brother Ignacio is the only one left. So is his only son. His daughter was taken away and is probably dead now. Luna once told me that the villages of the Tawahka were once many, with tens of thousands of people.

Today, this is the only one and she said it gets smaller every time she comes."

I noticed that Jorge continued speaking of his dead sister as if she were still alive and wondered if that was just their way, or if he still hadn't fully accepted the fact that his only sibling was gone.

The enormity of what he'd said hit me. Aldrick and Ignacio were the last of their family and Jorge was the last of the next generation of that same family. Out of the three Mejia siblings and two of their spouses—five people in all—Jorge was likely the only offspring to survive.

An ethnic group moving toward extinction.

Aldrick and his brother returned with the rest of the hunting party, as well as with a number of women and girls.

"Three men arrived in the truck just after noon and went up into the hills without supplies or carriers."

"Carriers?" I asked.

"They hire men from the village to carry the supplies up and bring the cocaine back."

"What for?" Axel asked. "Why do your people tolerate them?"

Aldrick turned toward my helmsman as the women picked up the bundles and started off with them.

"The people are very poor," Aldrick said. "And the men are very few, and not permitted to have guns."

Axel and Ross both looked at the young man carrying the old carbine.

Aldrick shrugged. "He breaks the law."

"So, what do we do until they leave?" I asked.

Suddenly, there were shouts from the other side of the village.

"Stay here," he said. "They are returning."

Aldrick, his brother, and two of the other hunters turned and hurried off toward the village.

The man with the rifle stayed behind, unslinging it from his shoulder. He looked at me, uncertainty in his eyes, then turned a small log, exposing a wooden crate. He opened it, put his rifle inside, then rolled the log back over onto the spot before hurrying off after his comrades.

The six of us looked at one another.

"Who goes off to meet the enemy and leaves their weapon?" Ross asked nobody in particular.

Through the leaves fringing our hiding spot, we saw two Hispanic men coming out of the forest near where their truck was parked on the north side of the village. We waited, but no third man appeared. I scanned the edge of the forest, searching for him, but it was just the two.

The guys coming down from the other side of the village stopped and said something to a group of old women. One of them pointed toward the hunting party, which had skirted the back of the village and was following the stream toward the outsiders.

One of the Hispanic men stepped away and I heard him greet Ignacio by name. They talked for a few minutes, though we were too far away to hear, then Aldrick stepped forward. The outsider turned and Aldrick followed him. They rejoined the other man and all three started back toward the trail.

"Where the hell's he going?" Axel asked.

Once they were out of sight, Ignacio hurried back through the village toward us. As one, we rose from behind the log.

"*No pude detenerlo*," Ignacio said as he neared us.

"He said he couldn't stop him," Gerald translated.

"Ask him where they're taking him," I said.

145

Gerald did and Ignacio replied in rapid-fire Spanish.

"They didn't take him," Gerald said. "The cartel stooges needed someone good at tracking and the professor volunteered."

"We're following them," I said. "Duster, you're on point. Comms on."

All five of us retrieved communication devices from pockets and turned them on. I handed a spare to Jorge, then fitted mine in my left ear, showing him how to snug the bone mic around the outside of the ear.

"Comm check," I said.

The others responded and I heard them, then Duster nodded and hurried off, moving low and fast around the side of the village, taking cover where he could.

"*El bosque es peligroso para ti,*" Ignacio said, telling us that the forest was a dangerous place for us.

"*Somos los peligrosos en el bosque,*" Gerald told him, then hurried off after Duster.

He was right—*we* were the dangerous ones in the forest.

The hunter who'd left the rifle in the box came up alongside Ignacio.

I looked at him, then glanced down at the branch hiding the box. "*Con permisso, por favor?*"

The man looked at Ignacio for guidance and the leader nodded.

Quickly, the young hunter rolled the log aside and opened the box. He removed the rifle and handed it to me, along with a loaded magazine.

I took the rifle and looked it over quickly. It was an old British Army issue Lee-Metford .303 caliber bolt-action. The Brits had used it as their primary infantry weapon for over a hundred years, though today, it was a ceremonial rifle. This one wasn't and it was probably manufactured in the early 1900s, if I had to guess.

Another magazine was in it, and it slid out easily when I pressed the release. I noted there were eight rounds in each. Definitely built before the First World War since later models held ten. When I opened the bolt, the chamber was empty. I pointed the barrel down and peered into the chamber. There was a little rust around the lip and on the extractor, but in such a wet environment, it was surprisingly clean.

I dropped the spare mag in my pocket, inserted the other one, then closed the bolt, loading a round into the chamber. "*Gracias,*" I said to the young man, then the three of us took off after Gerald, who was searching inside the cab of the Toyota.

"Paperwork in the glove box says it's owned by someone in San Pedro Sula," he said, closing the door. "Carlos Montoya."

CHAPTER TWENTY-TWO

Aldrick walked between the two men as they went up the trail from the village. He'd had a good idea of what it was they wanted him to track. That's why he'd volunteered over his brother. The two cartel men had accepted that he was a member of the village without question—just another invisible old man in the forest.

They'd been on the trail for ten minutes when the lead man turned onto the new trail that had been cut just a week earlier. The same trail on which he'd watched the man being killed by the jaguar.

Aldrick then had no doubt what they needed a tracker for. They wanted him to trail the *hombre gato*—the cat man—who brought the fierce jaguar down on their soldiers.

The irony didn't escape Aldrick.

He was at home in the dense rainforest—he a part of it and it a part of him, going back thousands of generations. These men weren't.

He could easily guide them straight to a jaguar mother's den, pretending he was tracking himself, then disappear like the mist.

"Is it far?" Aldrick asked in accented Spanish, like the indigenous people he was a blood part of. "I am an old man and tire easily."

"Not far," the man behind him said.

Aldrick turned to glance at him, then quickly brought his eyes back to the trail. He'd seen someone behind them. It was one of the younger men in Captain McDermitt's group, the one they called Duster.

The captain and his men didn't act like any mariners Aldrick had ever met. And Jorge spoke highly of the organization they represented. The man following them had moved more like a soldier than a sailor, ducking for cover instantly when Aldrick turned around.

And he was armed.

Aldrick realized that he could deal with these *narcotraficantes* another way, so as not to endanger the mother jaguar and her cubs. He smiled inwardly. The Americans were following the cartel. He would lead them straight to the clearing where the cartel grew the coca. He'd scouted it before. There were only a handful of armed men there.

They continued along the barely discernable trail hacked through the forest. Aldrick knew where they were and where they were going. It was only a few more minutes, just around the next bend in the trail.

When they reached it, Aldrick expected to see the third man, but nobody was around.

"This is it, right, Carlos?" the lead man said.

The man named Carlos stepped past him and looked around before pointing to the roots of the giant ceiba tree Aldrick had hidden behind two nights earlier.

"That is the tree," Carlos said. "Where is El Astilla?"

The sliver? Aldrick thought. He'd said it as if it was someone's name. Was that the third man his brother said had arrived in the truck?

Aldrick had heard the stories about the man known only as El Astilla, the Cholóma cartel's number one enforcer—the man he was certain had killed Luna.

Aldrick felt the weight of the small box in his pocket. He could easily drop one of the fragile vials onto a rock and, if there was a jaguar within a mile, it would soon start moving this way. And in the Río Plátano Biosphere, the jaguar population all but ensured one would be nearby, perhaps even watching them now.

He scanned the trees, where the great cats liked to wait.

"What are you looking for, old man?" a voice from the mist asked.

Aldrick jumped, his head jerking in the direction the trail led. A man rose from behind a large rock. He wore a hat, low over his eyes, and a long coat that nearly reached his ankles.

Carlos took a step toward the man. "For a minute, I thought one of those cats got you."

"Who is this man?" the one Aldrick assumed was El Astilla demanded.

"My name is Roderigo Mejia," Aldrick said, using his dead brother-in-law's first name. "I am Ignacio's brother and a much better tracker than he."

"You are?" the man asked. "How good?"

Aldrick looked past him, studying the trail beyond. He could see where the man had walked up and down it, though he'd left little sign.

"You went up the trail, staying to one side, for about a stone's throw," Aldrick said, then pointed. "You returned on the other side and stopped to urinate next to that trumpet tree."

El Astilla turned and looked up the trail. When he looked back, he smiled. But Aldrick saw no humor in the man's dark, brooding eyes.

"You are good," he said. "But you didn't answer my question. What were you looking for?"

Aldrick scanned the lower tree limbs again. "The *yaguara* waits in the trees for his dinner to come to him."

El Astilla's eyes flicked up to the trees for a moment, then he waved a hand for Aldrick to follow him. "Come look over here, Roderigo."

They went over to the spot where Aldrick had lain in wait for the men to come back from the coca field. None of the villagers would go up there at night to carry for them, so the cartel had brought their own people that night.

"What do you see here?" El Astilla asked.

Aldrick moved around the winding wood walls the roots created, pretending to study the ground. From the corner of his eye, he could see Duster, peering at them from between thick leaves, no more than twenty meters away.

"One man," Aldrick said. "Not an animal. You brought me here to track a man?"

"Not just any man," El Astilla said. "This man moves like a ghost, leaving no sign."

Aldrick decided he needed to play up his part a little. There was still some doubt in the man's eyes.

He turned to face the killer. "I will not track a man for you," he said. "Not for just one thousand lempira."

The man's hand moved, parting his coat to reveal the ornate hilt of a machete. He rested his hand lightly on it. "I could kill you right here."

"Yes, you can," Aldrick said, remaining firm. "But I am old anyway, and then you will have nobody to track this man."

"Two thousand," El Astilla offered.

"Three."

Aldrick knew that men like these always carried thousands of lempira. Three thousand wouldn't buy a textbook.

The man smiled at him. "Twenty-five hundred."

Aldrick nodded and extended a hand.

"Pay him," El Astilla said to Carlos.

The other man dug into his pockets and pulled out a roll of bills, peeling off five *quinientos* lempira notes and extending his hand to Aldrick.

He took the cash and stuffed it into his pocket with the vials full of the mixture he'd created. When he'd discovered that biologists were spraying their motion sensor cameras with a certain men's cologne to attract jaguars, he learned what the ingredients were. The binder that held the other parts of the cologne mixture together was a derivative of civet oil, called civetone. His "cologne" contained that, as well as the blood and urine from a deer. The jaguars he'd tested it on found even a single drop of it to be irresistible and could smell it from a great distance.

"The man you seek was here two nights ago," Aldrick said to El Astilla. "He stayed for a long time, perhaps two nights."

"Was a jaguar with him?" Carlos asked.

"A jaguar?" Aldrick said, turning to face the other two. "No, the man was here alone." Then he pointed up the hill beyond the ceiba tree. "The great cat came from up there." He walked over to where he knew the animal had passed his lair and easily found a partial track. He knelt next to it. "The cat passed by him and went down to the trail."

Carlos looked from where Aldrick knelt to the place he'd once hidden, just four meters away. "It walked right past him? Without knowing he was there?"

"Or perhaps it is like you said, Carlos," the third man said. "*El Hombre Gato* summoned the cat."

"Don't talk stupid, Demian," El Astilla said. "A man cannot summon a wild jaguar. The man who hid here was quiet, the men on the trail noisy. Nothing more."

"What if it isn't wild?" Demian said, defending his position.

El Astilla knelt beside Aldrick and looked at the slight impression in the leaves. "Yes, I see it now." He rose and looked down at Aldrick. "Pay no attention to that *idiota*. Where did the man go?"

CHAPTER TWENTY-THREE

With Gerald leading the way, we started up the jungle trail after Duster. Ross brought up the rear, keeping an eye out behind us. The forest quickly enveloped us, and I had that same eerie feeling that time was suspended.

The trail was well worn, probably the main artery from the village to long-dormant crop fields or hunting grounds. Or maybe it connected this village with another—a trade route. The ground was covered with a dense, spongy carpet of decaying vegetation, and our footfalls were absorbed by it and the forest around us.

Normally, a fire team would move up a trail in a staggered formation, with the fire team leader and a rifleman on one side of the road and the automatic rifleman and his loader on the other. But we stayed to the outside of each turn, changing sides often as the trail twisted and turned, following the landscape.

Twice, Duster warned us that there was a switchback and Aldrick and the two cartel thugs would be passing above us. We had to stop and wait until they'd passed, then hurry up the trail to a near 180-degree turn.

After quite some time, Duster's whispered voice came over my earwig. "They turned down an unmarked side trail to the left. Leaving a sign."

"Roger the first breadcrumb," Gerald said.

We hurried on, knowledgeable of the fact that Duster was between us and the men we were following.

"Here," Gerald said, pointing to a long, slender leaf lying on the trail.

Normally, a leaf on the forest floor wouldn't be unusual, just one of millions of others, but this one was green and freshly cut. It pointed to a shadow of an opening through the dense foliage.

"The professor spotted me," Duster whispered.

"Get small," Gerald said. "We're turning off the main trail."

Gerald tossed the leaf into the bushes, where it was less conspicuous, and we moved out. Another hour passed as we climbed. We moved fast, but as quietly as possible. Gerald could actually see Duster from time to time and we trusted that he could see our adversaries.

Finally, Duster's whispered voice came over the com. "They've stopped. The third man was waiting for them. They're talking. Going silent to try to get closer. Leaving another sign."

"Roger on the second breadcrumb," Gerald said.

From there, we started moving slower, not wanting to alert the bad guys. We picked our way up the trail carefully, with Gerald looking for the second marker. We were ready for any eventuality and getting Aldrick back was the priority.

I had no idea what the antique rifle was zeroed at. Not that it mattered a whole lot in the forest. The maximum distance I could see was less than a hundred yards, and the old .303's trajectory was probably flat at that distance.

The front sight was fixed, and the rear sight wedge was less than a fourth of the way up the slide, which meant it was probably sighted for short range—a hundred yards, which seemed logical, given the conditions in which it was being used. The rear sight was also adjustable laterally for windage. Whatever wind blew this far inland, it remained up above the canopy, more than a hundred feet over our heads. I had only felt a light breeze while in the village. The windage dope was just slightly off-center. I had to assume the young villager knew how to adjust his sights and it was off-center to bring the point of impact onto the line of sight in zero wind conditions. A hundred years of being bumped around could easily have it off.

I carried the rifle with the muzzle down, the safety off, and my index finger extended alongside the trigger guard. I felt comfortable that I could have the stock welded against my cheek in a micro-second and a round on target in less than a heartbeat. I'd trained Marine infantrymen, particularly scout/snipers, for many years.

After the first round was away, racking the bolt could take only slightly longer than a semi-automatic to reload and fire again, if the shooter was familiar with the weapon, which I wasn't. Every bolt, even on similar weapons, was unique—each had its own movement and slide friction. And even on the same rifle, it could vary, depending on maintenance. I'd only opened and closed the bolt once on that particular rifle. Still, it had felt smooth, but I doubted I could get eight shots off accurately in under ten seconds with it, like I could with my old M40. Maybe with the second magazine, I could. But a sniper's mission isn't to send as many rounds as he can send downrange. It's about where those bullets impact.

Ahead, Gerald raised a fist and got low. We all stopped and crouched in the foliage. He looked back and signaled that four men were ahead. I silently moved up to join him, peering through a gap in a group of large elephant ear leaves.

The professor and his two escorts had finally met up with the third man Ignacio had reported going up into the hills before we'd arrived at the village. I had no idea what they wanted with Aldrick or why the third man had remained when the other two went back down. He didn't seem hurt. Their body language told me the third man, the one who'd waited and wore a low hat and long coat, was the boss.

I cupped my hand over my mouth and whispered, "Tangoes in sight, Duster."

His response was equally quiet. "I'm twenty-five yards to Gerald's ten o'clock."

With the bone mics fitted tight against the jaw hinge, they could pick up spoken words that a person couldn't hear when whispered from just inches away.

Gerald turned his head in that direction, searching the dense forest. The two men had worked together a lot, in training and on the battlefield. It showed in the way they communicated and moved.

"Got you," he whispered. "What are they doing?"

"The professor is pointing up the trail," Duster whispered. "They want him to track a man who was there two nights ago."

I pulled Jorge close. "Do you know what's up that trail?"

He shook his head. "Not for certain. The coca field, I would guess. This area was where the most recent jaguar attack happened."

"Stay on them," Duster. "We'll follow behind you."

We remained in position for a good three minutes before Gerald raised his fist and pumped it twice.

Continuing quietly, we made our way up the trail, a lot more slowly this time. Gerald could see Duster from time to time, and

Duster was moving at the same pace as Aldrick and the three men. Slower was good. Slow was smooth and smooth was fast.

If the professor were tracking a man, or even an animal, he wouldn't be moving very fast. Tracking was a slow, arduous process, finding one sign, aligning it with a previous one to guess where the quarry would move next, then concentrating on that area before moving toward it, always cognizant of the ground in-between, where a hidden sign might be found. Tracking wasn't about speed—often the quarry was moving much faster than the tracker. It was more about precision and stamina. Eventually, the prey had to stop and rest.

Even Jorge seemed to be more alert, no longer creating so much noise. I checked my watch. It would be dark in less than two hours.

Locating where the men had stopped was easy. They'd found the exact spot of the jaguar attack. Whoever the man had been, he'd lost a lot of blood in a very short time. Arterial spray reached leaves above eye level.

We continued upward, basically blind. Gerald kept Duster in sight, and we were spread out behind the old infantry master sergeant. This decreased the likelihood of our being heard or spotted while we relied on Duster to follow the men who had Aldrick. He was very good at it.

Suddenly, I heard a shouted voice from way up the trail. *"Parada! Quién eres tú?"*

"Get small," Duster ordered needlessly, accenting it with a grunt as he hit the ground.

Gerald dove to his left and I went right, pulling Jorge down beside me. I didn't have to look back to know that Axel had moved to the left side of the trail and Ross to the right, facing aft. We were all in a defensive position facing outboard.

Jorge, not being an infantryman, simply knelt on the ground, looking around. But he did finally pull a sidearm from under his shirt.

I got his attention, pointed two fingers at my eyes, then at Gerald and Axel. Then I pointed to myself and moved my hand in an arc pointing from Gerald, at the twelve o'clock position of our group, to the jungle at three o'clock. Pointing to him, I assigned him three to six.

He nodded his understanding and took up position beside me, gun at the ready.

"What's going on?" I asked quietly.

There was no reply.

A moment later, Duster whispered, "Checkpoint."

I could hear someone ahead replying to the sentry's challenge. "*Es* Carlos Montoya. *Estamos entrando.*"

"How many guards, Duster?" I asked.

"One," he replied. "He's passing them through."

"Can you take him out?" I asked. "He's probably guarding the coca farm and lab."

I said the last part to give Duster justification. We were no longer in the military, nor working directly for the government, as I had with Homeland Security. We were private citizens at best, hired mercenaries at worst. We didn't have a problem with that. Having a badge on your chest or chevrons on your sleeve didn't make a man right. He wore those things because of what did—some innate sense of justice.

"Roger that," Duster replied.

And that was it. I'd asked him to kill a man and he'd agreed. Justice didn't always come from a court bench.

We waited quietly for several minutes, and then I heard a grunt and the sound of a struggle. It ceased almost as quickly as it had started.

"One tango down," Duster said. "The edge of a large field is just ahead of me."

"Who are you people?" Jorge asked, turning to look at me.

"Just a bunch of boat bums and oceanographers," I replied. "Gerald, move out."

As one, we rose and hurried up the trail. We found Duster by a crudely built shelter. A dead man sat on a stump leaning against the guard shack, his lifeless eyes staring up at the rainforest canopy. Duster picked up the man's AK-47 and checked it over.

Then he turned to me and nodded. I nodded back. The spoils of war go to the victor. Duster was now the proud owner of a new automatic rifle.

Peering around the thatch-covered lean-to, I could see the field. It was coca, all right. The broad, oval leaves and red berries caught the late evening sun. We were on the southwest side of a field that was probably twenty acres. Workers were making their way toward a cluster of small buildings on the far side.

"Spread out," I said. "Watch the tree line for any other guards or trails in."

Ross and Axel veered to the left and Duster and Gerald to the right. I let my eyes roam around the field, identifying every movement, but I didn't see anyone except the field workers, the professor, and the men who'd brought him there. I assumed work was done for the day and the workers were heading in to get their evening meal and rest for tomorrow.

"Nothing," Gerald said, after a few minutes. "Not even another trail. I'm halfway around this side."

"Same here," Axel said.

"These locations are secret," Jorge said. "As are the trails. I wouldn't think there would be more than one."

The three men with Aldrick were moving directly through the field toward the buildings, following the workers.

I looked more closely at the buildings. One was little more than a large field tent, probably where the men slept. Nobody was near it.

The second structure was a bit more permanent but had a thatched roof like the guard shack. A thin trail of smoke rose through an opening at the top. The kitchen and eating area, no doubt. There was a man with an assault rifle similar to the one Duster now carried posted in front of it. He watched the workers coming in but hadn't yet seen the man I now knew as Carlos Montoya, his men, and the professor.

The third building was made of rough, unpainted wood. It had a metal roof, which shone brightly in the gathering dusk—brand new. They must have flown all the materials in by chopper. There was no way all that could be carried up here on that so-called trail. There were two men outside what I assumed was the lab—each armed with an AK like the others.

In my head, without thinking, I created a shooting solution. The smoke told me there was no wind and the distance was no more than two hundred yards to the guards at the lab. The coca plants themselves were unmoving—not a puff of wind between me and them. The guards stood on either side of the door, occasionally talking. It was easier to walk a bolt action to the left, so the guard on the right was my first target.

The field itself would provide great cover for the others to get closer, as the plants were half-grown, standing a good four feet tall.

"Anyone see more than three weapons?" I asked.

Gerald was first to answer. "I'd assume the three with the professor are armed."

"Move into the field," I ordered. "Get within accurate distance. I'll take out the two guards from here and can warn you if anyone moves back toward the field. Duster, you get the guard at the kitchen. The rest of you get the men with Professor Mejia—coordinate left to right. Let me know when you're in position."

It was at least six of them against the six of us, three rifles to two. We were actually five, since Jorge was with me and way out of range for his pistol. But we had the setting sun partly at our backs, great cover to get close completely undetected, and the element of surprise was all ours.

Was it cold-blooded murder? In my mind, I didn't see it that way. These men were armed and dangerous. They'd taken to a life of crime and violence. I knew how these cartels worked. The men who were about to die today had each gone through a number of rituals to prove themselves—crimes that would carry a death sentence in any just society. I had no more compunction about killing them than I would have stepping on a roach in *Ambrosia's* galley.

A man wearing some sort of hazmat suit came out of what was obviously the lab. The men with Aldrick angled toward him. The man in the long coat and hat, along with one of the others, approached the guy in the hazmat suit and they talked.

One by one, my men reported they were in position. When they were all ready, I instructed them to open fire as soon as they heard my first shot. Duster had moved a lot closer, knowing, as I did, that the AK was notoriously inaccurate. He was less than fifty yards from the kitchen and in a prone position with a clear line of sight. Still, I trusted the antique British rifle a lot more than the Russian-made AK.

The others—Gerald, Axel, and Ross—were spread out, just inside the field. We were undetected and ready.

I remained in a standing position, leaning against a tree, and spreading my legs. I brought the rifle up, subconsciously looping my arm through the sling. I welded the stock to my cheek and shoulder and took aim. From two hundred yards, if I were using my M40 with a scope, I could drive nails into a tree, so a head shot would have been my preference. But with an untested rifle and iron sights, I aimed for high center mass.

The rifle bucked in my hands and time slowed as I felt the familiar recoil, not all that different from my own M40. I racked the bolt, acquired the second target, and fired at a spot low and right, before the first guard even began to fall. When he did, the second guard started to move toward him, right into the path of my second bullet. They both went down.

The field suddenly erupted in gunfire. In seconds, it was over—all three armed men in the camp as well as the three who were with Aldrick went down. The workers fled into the forest on the east side of the field, arms high over their heads.

Only Aldrick Mejia and the man in the hazmat suit remained standing. He raised his gloved hands high over his head.

Aldrick slowly turned toward the field with a satisfied look on his face. He stood calmly as we approached, hands clasped in front, as if he were waiting for his class to take their seats.

Gerald and the others fanned out, clearing all three buildings as Jorge and I strode quickly through the field toward Aldrick.

Ross pulled the mask off the man in the white protective suit and pushed him down to his knees at gunpoint, forcing him to lace his fingers behind his head.

"Are you okay?" I asked, as we came out of the field into the camp.

"I am fine," he replied. "One of them got away."

I'd seen all six men go down, practically at the same time. But when I looked around, only the three armed men from the camp and the two men who'd taken Aldrick away from the village lay on the ground. The man with the hat and long coat wasn't there.

"Where'd the guy in the hat go?" I asked.

"He disappeared," was Aldrick's only reply.

Jorge stepped closer to his uncle. "Who was he?"

"He was the man known as El Astilla," Aldrick replied. "The man who killed your sister."

CHAPTER TWENTY-FOUR

There were numerous five-gallon containers of acetone in the lab, along with other chemicals. I had Ross, Axel, and Duster carry them out to the center of the field. I told them to slosh the acetone around in a ten- foot circle, then leave them uncapped in the middle. Then I had Duster carry one back, leaving a trail of acetone on the ground all the way into the lab.

I took a burning log from the cook fire and ignited the acetone trail in the middle. A blue flame raced from the end of my burning log in both directions until it reached the open containers. There was a whoosh of flame as fumes in the containers erupted, spraying most of the field and the inside of the lab with flaming liquid.

"You'd have made a good science professor," Aldrick said.

"What were you doing, leading them up here?" I asked, as the chemical flames died quickly, leaving the plants and building ablaze.

"I intended to lead them into the forest to kill them," he replied, his face a blank slate. "Then I saw your man following us and decided I could use you to wipe out this farm."

I glared at him for a moment. "You willfully put my people in jeopardy?"

"I saw the way you and your men acted on the trail as we went down to my village," he said. "I think that in another life, you were a jaguar. I coupled that with what Jorge told me about your organization and decided that the only ones in jeopardy were the cartel people."

That the man had a brilliant mind, I had no doubt. Scholars speaking to the General Assembly of the UN had to have some serious chops. The fact that he could apply his intelligence to a tactical situation was intriguing.

"And the man who got away?" I asked.

"He is called El Astilla—The Sliver. He is one of the cartel's top *sicarios*, or paid assassins. He moves well in the forest. I think he is an *indígena* or mixed race and he has spent much time in the forest. These two men were cartel lieutenants and did not know the forest at all."

He knew a lot for someone who hadn't been in this part of the world for ten years. I doubted that he'd learned it by chatting with them on the hike up from the village.

"What about this guy?" Gerald asked, standing beside the lab worker. "And the ones who took off into the jungle?"

"The others are nothing," Aldrick said, as the flames dwindled. "Simple farm workers from neighboring villages forced to work the coca fields. They will return to their villages." He turned toward the lab worker. "I would assume this man was sent here by the cartel."

I pulled the man's hair, turning his face upward. "*Trabajas para el cartel de* Cholóma ?"

He twisted his head, glaring at me with a violence he hadn't exhibited before. "Yes, I do," he replied in English. "And all of you, and all of your families, will *die* before the week ends."

I drew my Sig and shot him in the head. "It won't be you who tells them, *amigo*." I turned back to Aldrick, who had a stunned expression on his face. "Can you track El Astilla?"

He looked up from the dead man. "What?"

"Can you track him?"

"He'll probably go back to the village," Gerald said. "Then take the truck back over to Chológma ."

"Maybe not," I said, not taking my eyes off Aldrick's. "If he is indigenous, like the professor thinks, he may try to get there on foot, or more likely, make his way somewhere else. That's what I'd do if someone was chasing me in the Everglades."

"Yes," Aldrick said, nodding, "I can track him."

"We can't let him get away," I told the man. "If he does, the cartel will take this out on your village."

"I will do this," Aldrick said. "And when we catch him, I will be the one to cut his heart out."

Aldrick Mejia wasn't some mild-mannered college professor. He was one of the last of his kind, a leader among a group of people struggling to regain their identity while their numbers teetered on the edge of extinction.

The fire had spread to the kitchen structure but had quickly burnt itself out in the moisture-rich air. Acetone is a highly flammable liquid and doesn't burn long.

I glanced toward the western sky, taking a few steps toward the field. The heat from the fire drew cool, damp air in from the surrounding forest, bringing a heavy mist low to the ground. The mist moved like liquid, heavier than the surrounding air, following the contour of the landscape. We were close to four thousand feet above sea level, maybe higher. Though the air was cool, it was thin and very humid, the reason for the ever-present mist.

Each breath was a labor.

The sun was already below the trees and a crescent moon was only a couple of hours behind it. Not that it would make any difference if it were a full moon directly overhead. In the jungle it would be almost utter blackness.

"It'll be dark soon," I said.

Gerald nodded. "He'll have to stop and find a place to spend the night." He unslung his pack, tugged it open, and pulled out a pair of single-tube night-vision goggles. "We won't have to stop."

"What is that?" Mejia asked.

It was an unexpected question, since night-vision optics weren't a big secret and the professor, though he came from a primitive tribe, was highly educated and I assumed, no stranger to technology. Anything the military had could be purchased right online. If you had deep pockets.

"The latest from ATN," Gerald said. "NVG7, third-generation night- vision optics."

"Is it easy to use?"

Gerald grinned up at him. "So easy, a caveman can do it."

A slow smile spread across the man's face as he reached for the goggles. "Show me how it works."

"How did he just up and disappear?" Axel asked.

Aldrick stopped and looked around. "He was behind me when the shooting started." He turned toward the lab and knelt by the door, where smoke was still rising out of the smoldering interior. After examining the narrow space between the floor of the lab and the ground, he said, "I heard him fall. He must have gone under the building."

Just to make sure, Axel got down on his belly and shined the light from his cell phone under the lab.

"Nothing," he said. "But it does look like someone crawled under here in a big hurry."

Aldrick walked around the building. At the back, he paused and knelt down. "Here is where he came out."

Rising, he looked all around in the gathering gloom, eyes sweeping the ground from left to right and back again.

"There," he said, pointing. He moved cautiously toward the edge of the forest, then knelt again. "He came this way. Follow me."

"Here," Gerald said, extending the goggles toward Aldrick. "It's already turned on. Just fit it over your eyes and pull the straps tight."

"I will carry them for now," Aldrick said. "How long will the battery last?"

Gerald grinned. "All night. And the next three nights, at least."

Aldrick looked down at the device in his hand. "Amazing."

Somehow, his simple statement and action seemed contrived to me, as if he wanted Gerald to believe he'd never heard of such technology.

We moved out, back into the primordial rainforest as night closed in around us. With just a few steps in, it was noticeably darker. A few more, and all color disappeared. Aldrick was nothing but a moving gray shape in front of me.

"Stay close," I said to the others. "Move slow. No lights. No sound. When the moon sets in two hours, we'll be lucky if we don't bump into one another."

"Or a hungry jaguar on the hunt," Ross added.

It didn't take long for the darkness to envelop us. The night sounds in the rainforest were totally different from those of the day. Only predators ventured out at night. Predators with very good eyesight.

Aldrick led the way, stopping every few feet and scanning the rugged terrain ahead. He put the goggles on and forged ahead. To say it was dark would be an understatement. Whenever Aldrick stopped, he became invisible to me.

I'd slung my rifle and changed to the Sig. There was too much of a chance I'd bang the barrel against a tree if I had to turn and aim quickly. Not that I could see anything to aim at.

Finally, Aldrick stopped and knelt behind a deadfall. As I crept slowly up behind him, I saw him take something from his pocket and appeared to throw it up ahead of him. But with virtually no light, it was hard to say.

I came up beside him, the others right behind me, as if they'd been holding one another's shirttails.

"What do you see?" I whispered.

"We have found El Astilla. Now we must be very silent and wait."

I took the night-vision goggles from Aldrick and held them to my eyes as I looked over the giant log. The optics were top of the line and very expensive. The depth of field was a few inches to infinity, allowing a person to read a map or make notes, then look at something in the distance with a clarity other devices tried to measure up to. It was still shades of gray-green, but the sharpness over even color night-vision was amazing.

Movement caught my eye. A man tucked into a crevice between two massive rocks moved his legs. It was the man with the hat, but he now had it resting on his lap. In his right hand, he held a machete, the blade resting across his chest.

I lowered the NVGs and looked over at Aldrick. Even inches away, I could barely see his face. The others were just shadows around us.

"Why wait?" I asked. "It looks like he has nothing but a machete."

"We will wait for the forest," Aldrick said. "But we must be extremely silent."

"What was that I saw you throw?" I asked him.

Just then, I heard a kind of chuffing sound coming from beyond and to the south of where the man huddled in the crevice about a hundred feet away.

"Silence," Aldrick warned.

CHAPTER TWENTY-FIVE

When the first rifle shot split the air, Gustavo Ramos had started moving, even before the guard had fallen. He'd hit the ground and rolled to the side of the building as more gunfire erupted, scraping his way through the loose leaves until he was under the building. He'd scrambled quickly between two floor joists to the other side, where he'd pushed and clawed at the leaves and dirt to get out.

Gustavo had been born in a small village near the coast, in eastern Honduras. When he'd been old enough to understand, his mother, a Miskito woman, told him that she'd never known who his father was—he was just one of many Hispanic men from the nearby town of Limón who'd captured and gang-raped young Miskito girls on a regular basis.

Later, as a boy, he'd often gone with the men of his village, traveling deep into the forest to kill game. Even then, he'd had a natural intuition and could track animals as well as many of the seasoned hunters.

Once he'd regained his feet, Gustavo had wasted no time and quietly disappeared into the forest with the field workers. Most of them had fled east but he continued north, away from the coca field and higher up the mountain.

He had no idea who it was who'd attacked the farm. It could be a rival cartel—it happened sometimes—or maybe the police. Either way, he wasn't waiting around to find out.

Two explosions behind him urged Gustavo on, spurring him deeper into the forest. He didn't think a rival cartel would blow up the lab. They'd simply take it over, finish processing what plants had grown, and take off with the cocaine.

If it was the police, they'd burn the field, but not before gathering evidence from the lab, and that would take some time.

Whoever they were, their attack on the farm owned by Señora Paloma would bring down swift retribution once he reported it. But first, he would have to make his way to a nearby Miskito village many kilometers to the north, near the sea.

Night was falling and Gustavo had no food or water. He moved northward as fast as he could go in the low light afforded by the rainforest canopy. He knew he'd find water, and a night without food wouldn't kill him.

He would find a place to hide out when it got dark. He knew how inhospitable the forest was at night, but he wasn't afraid; being out in the open, unable to see an approaching threat, was simply stupid.

The attackers wouldn't pursue the escaping workers for very far, and he was going in an entirely different direction. He was safe from them, but not from the forest. At least not at night.

He would find water first. And in these mountains, where there was running water, he knew there would be large rocks.

He quickly put several kilometers between him and the burning buildings; the glow from the fires disappeared rapidly. He pushed on in the near-total darkness, occasionally tripping over a branch or vine.

Finally, he came to a place where summer rains had cut a wide chasm, leaving many underlying boulders exposed. The sometimes-raging stream was now nothing but a trickle. He knelt and drank from his hands, and then moved upstream and soon found what he was looking for—a crack in the rocks large enough for him to fit inside.

Gustavo moved some smaller stones out of the way and tucked his body into the crack, but not before pulling one of his blades out.

He sat down on the ground, knees tucked close to his chest as he held the blade out toward the darkness.

After a while, he moved his legs, straightening them a little, put the machete across his chest and fell asleep.

Hearing something, Gustavo woke with a start. He had no idea how long he'd slept. It could have been minutes or hours—the darkness was absolute. Some sound had awakened him, but he could see nothing beyond the rocks, and tucked into the crevice where light didn't reach, he couldn't even see the bright, shiny blade in his hand.

The thin air inside his little crack began to take on a musky, putrid smell, one he'd smelled before, back on the trail where the carrier had been killed by the jaguar. As bad as it was, it wasn't the stink that concerned him.

There was something out there. He could hear slight noises and felt as if someone or something was watching him. He drew his legs up, ready to spring, pointing the blade back out toward the darkness again.

Suddenly, he heard a sound that turned his blood to ice and sent a shiver of fear throughout his body.

It was the soft chuff a jaguar made when on the hunt.

If he held perfectly still and didn't make a sound, the cat might move toward whatever else was there in the forest with him. He figured it must be one of the escaped workers, lost in the darkness.

"Silence," he heard a voice whisper out of the darkness.

He smiled inwardly. It was an *Americano*, perhaps one of those who'd attacked the farm—most likely American DEA agents. With that one word, whoever it was had sealed their fate. The nearby jaguar would soon kill them, and they would never see it coming.

All of a sudden, a great weight fell on top of Gustavo, knocking the machete aside as many daggers pierced his flesh, and a powerful force clamped down on the side of his head. He screamed and tried to struggle, but the pain in the side of his head was excruciating.

There was a sudden crunching sound, and everything went to a deeper, darker blackness than Gustavo Ramos had ever experienced.

CHAPTER TWENTY-SIX

I slowly rose and put the goggles back to my eyes, my Sig leading them over the log. The man known as El Astilla was still there, but he seemed nervous and now had the machete pointing out toward the darkness. A smile slowly spread across his face, as if he knew that death itself had passed him by.

Without warning, something large dropped on top of the man and I watched in horror as the giant spotted cat took the man's head in its powerful jaws. He screamed, but it was cut off by an audible cracking sound as the jaguar's fangs punctured the man's skull and stilled his brain.

I'd read that the jaguar was able to kill much larger prey than itself, even the giant black caiman, largest of all the alligator species, by sinking its long fangs into its victim's skull and brain.

El Astilla's legs kicked out and spasmed twice, then his body went limp. The cat dragged it out of the crevice, then quickly eviscerated its hapless victim, instinctively going for the high iron content of any mammal—the liver and heart.

Everyone remained motionless and quiet as I slowly crouched back down. We could all hear the sound of the feeding jaguar. It was unhurried now; a short, fierce battle, and the quarry was dead.

Being that close was troubling, and it wasn't just the gruesome aspect of what we were hearing, though that sent shivers up and down my spine. The question was, what would happen when it finished feeding?

The jaguar was a part of the forest, the pinnacle of the food chain. It was the largest cat in the Americas and the third largest in the world. Only lions and tigers were bigger. They hunted mostly in the early hours of darkness or just before dawn, relying on natural night vision, a keen sense of smell, and excellent hearing.

The one that'd just killed El Astilla was every bit of two hundred pounds. With fangs and claws both exceeding two inches in length, the man never had a chance as it dropped from the rocks above him.

But we did have a chance. We had guns.

I didn't want to kill the jaguar if we didn't have to, but if it came down to the cat or one of my people, I'd drop it in a heartbeat.

Fortunately, it didn't come to that. We soon heard a dragging sound and I looked back over the log with the NVGs. The cat had the dead man's shoulder firmly clamped in a vice-like bite, holding its prize high as it dragged the man's carcass away into the jungle.

When I squatted back down, Aldrick was gone.

"Where'd the professor go?" I whispered harshly.

"What?" Jorge said, from a few feet away. "He was right here between you and me."

"Lights!" I said, standing and taking my satellite phone out.

A regular cell phone was of little use in the interior, where there were no towers, and with the heavy forest canopy overhead, there was no satellite phone reception either. But the satellite phones Armstrong had had privately manufactured had a very powerful light built in. In seconds, the others had theirs on and the forest was illuminated all around us for more than twenty yards.

Aldrick Mejia was nowhere to be seen.

"Where the hell did he go?" Gerald said, looking around.

I used the NVGs, aided by the lights, to search deeper into the jungle around us.

He'd vanished.

"Let's get back to the village," I said. "We can't do anything more here."

"You're just going to leave him out here?" Jorge asked.

"Nobody's leaving anyone, except your uncle," I said. "We'll be lucky to find our way back and I get the feeling he's in no danger in this jungle at all."

"He accomplished what he'd set out to do," Axel said. "Except he wanted to be the one who killed that guy."

"He did," I said. "What he said was, he wanted to cut out the heart of the man who'd killed Luna. I saw him throw something at that guy when he first saw him, and we all crouched behind this log."

"He didn't have a jaguar in his pocket," Gerald said. "That's what that was, wasn't it?"

"Yeah, it was a jaguar," I replied. "A big one. And Professor Mejia somehow attracted it to the man."

"That's impossible," Ross said. "Even domestic cats can't be trained to do very much. They just don't want to be."

"Whatever he threw brought that cat in like a laser-guided smart bomb." I stepped past them, taking the lead. "Let's go."

◆ ◆ ◆

It was midnight by the time we got back to the village. Ignacio was sitting beside a smoldering cook fire when we entered the low glow of light it provided. He rose and came quickly toward us. Gerald told him what had happened in the forest.

In the clearing, I was able to get a signal on my satellite phone. My first call was to Matt on *Ambrosia*.

"I was hopin' to 'ear from ya, Cap'n," he said. "It ain't like you to go so long without checkin' in."

"No signal under the forest canopy," I said. "Is everything okay there?"

"Oye," he replied. "I'm on watch on the bridge, mind. Mr. Meachum's down in the cockpit. Wasson?"

"We found a cocaine lab and field," I said. "Seven tangoes down, and the lab and field burned. I'm worried about retribution from the cartel on the villagers."

"What can I do to help?"

"Is Roger Tanaka in the op center?"

"Oye, been there most of the evenin'."

"Have him find out what Armstrong assets are nearby. We might need a little help."

"I'll get 'im right on it, Cap'n. Anything else?"

"Tell Savannah we're okay," I replied. "And have Roger call me when he finds out." I ended the call.

Gerald and Jorge were talking to Ignacio. I caught a little of what was being said. They were explaining how Aldrick had disappeared in the forest, but Ignacio's body language told me he wasn't all that concerned.

Finally, Gerald came over to where I stood, looking up at the night sky and working out a plan in my head.

"Ignacio says not to worry about his brother," Gerald said, his voice low. "Said he's more at home out there than he ever was up in New England."

"I can understand that," I said. "He was born to a primitive tribe. It's in his genes."

"Do you really think he somehow summoned that jaguar?"

I turned and looked at my number two security man. "I'm absolutely certain of it."

"But that part about cutting the guy's heart out? False bravado?"

"You've seen big cats feed," I said. "The first thing they go for is the heart and liver."

"Ahh," Gerald said, understanding what the professor had done. "He was speaking metaphorically. I wonder how he did it."

"Some sort of chemical bomb or something," I replied. "It was very small, no bigger than a .45 round. I saw him take it out of his pocket and throw it. Five minutes later, the jaguar appeared and took care of his wet work."

Just then my sat phone vibrated. I looked at the screen, expecting it to be Roger, but Deuce Livingston's name was there.

"Deuce?" I asked, after stabbing the *Talk* button. "What the hell are you doing calling so late?"

"Roger Tanaka called me," my friend said. "He told me you might need a hand."

"You're in Honduras?"

"Not exactly," he replied. "Give me your numbers; we can be there within a few hours."

Deuce was more than just a friend. I'd served with his dad and later, worked with Deuce's covert DHS team in South Florida. And now we both worked for Armstrong.

"Who's we?" I asked him.

"Just some old friends who want to drop in on you."

183

I used the satellite phone's GPS to get our location and explained to Deuce that we were in a small village in a valley on the Río Plátano.

"Perfect," Deuce said. "We're about to board an Armstrong jet in Nicaragua, headed back to the States. We can be over you in an hour or so."

I wasn't aware that he was in Central America, but I didn't have a need to know when it came to asset assignment. He'd tell me all about it later. However, parachuting from a corporate jet would be a new story—one that few men could tell.

"Can the village be used as a drop zone?" he asked.

I looked around. The houses were built well away from the river, probably above the high-water mark during the spring and fall monsoon seasons. From one end of the clearing to the other, it was several hundred yards long, sandy in the middle, but lined with rocks.

"Yeah," I replied. "It's clear for a little less than a quarter mile north to south, and wider than a football field. You have rigs?"

"Icarus rigs," he confirmed. "And we're fully armed. I even have a spare long gun for you. What about lights for the drop zone?"

I looked from one end of the village to the other. "There's a large cook fire a little north of center. That's my precise location. I'll light fires at the extreme ends, but the jungle canopy is a hundred feet high at the edge. It's gonna be a tight swoop."

"Any wind?"

"None to speak of," I replied. "An occasional light breeze from the north."

"Roger that," Deuce said. "Expect us in about an hour, two on the outside. I'll call you before we exit the aircraft."

I ended the call, wondering who Deuce had with him.

184

"Who was that?" Gerald asked.

"An old friend," I replied. "He and a few others are going to be dropping in soon. We need to turn this village into a drop zone."

"They're parachuting in?" he asked in disbelief. "Into the jungle at night?"

I grinned at the retired paratrooper. Although basically all similar, there were many ways of jumping out of an aircraft. Because the Army's 101st Airborne Division was huge, their troops were usually inserted from cargo planes, dropping out of the sky by the hundreds, and dangling below traditional round parachutes that had little maneuverable control, and typically into large fields during daylight hours. SEALs were a lot more covert when they jumped, usually in smaller numbers, and likely at night. Same with Marine Recon.

"We need fires marking the extreme ends and sides of the DZ," I said. "Twenty feet or so in from the tree line. Big fires. Bright enough to illuminate the treetops, especially at the south end."

"What do you have planned, Captain?" Axel asked.

I looked over at Ignacio, still standing beside the fire.

"We have a few more guests to invite," I replied, then turned to Gerald. "See if Ignacio knows of any of the villagers who are a little more than cozy with the Cholóma cartel. We need an information leak."

185

CHAPTER TWENTY-SEVEN

Thirty minutes after Gerald and Ignacio took a walk around the village, I saw someone come out of the back of one of the houses—the one Ignacio had identified as belonging to a man who often worked closely with the cartel bosses. He quickly disappeared up the road.

"Ignacio said it will only take him about an hour to reach that watering hole," Gerald said, when they returned from planting the seed for the invitation. "That place where we had to ford the stream. It's owned by a cartel member, and they sometimes use it as a meeting place."

"Then it's a pretty good bet that we were observed," I said. "The cartel has probably already been told that five Americans drove up here with two locals right after their three men came up."

"I made a point of boasting about killing all the cartel pukes," Gerald said. "And that we were planning to stay until we could get all the cocaine down from the farm."

"Good. Let's get busy turning this place into a drop zone."

Within an hour, we had fires set at all four corners of the village, with plenty of dry wood to throw on each when the time came.

Our wait wasn't long. At 0100 my phone vibrated in my pocket.

I took it out and answered it.

"We're ten minutes from the line of departure," Deuce said. "I called Chyrel, read her in, and asked for her help. She sounded excited. She has our comms on channel three via satellite. If you have line of sight, she should be able to loop you in."

"We have five fires going," I said. "They mark the center and outside corners. What altitude are you jumping from?"

"Thirty-five," he replied.

"Thirty-five hundred's kinda low, even for SEALs."

"Thirty-five thousand," he said. "We're making a HALO insertion, so Big Brother doesn't pick up the plane descending on radar. What's the ground elevation where you are?"

A HALO jump was made from high altitude, freefalling to a low opening altitude, sometimes just a thousand feet above the ground.

I opened the GPS on my phone and checked my current altitude.

"The center of the drop zone is 1,645 feet above sea level," I replied. "The south end is probably higher and the north end lower, but no more than ten feet. Mostly flat and sandy. The stream flows through the village lengthways, a little east of the middle, and there are rocks higher up the sides. You'll see the stream. Just stay close to it."

"Still no wind on the ground?"

I glanced over at the fire. Smoke and sparks were rising straight up in the night air. But higher, up above the trees, I could see it drifting to the south.

"Wind factor on the ground and up to about a hundred feet is zero," I replied. "But smoke from the fires is bending slightly to the south up above the treetops. I suggest you approach from that direction, even if it is a little downhill."

"Roger that," Deuce said. "We'll see you in a few minutes."

I picked up two small logs and tossed them into the already-blazing cook fire. "Add more wood to the fires," I said to the others over the com. "I'm switching channels, so talk to Gerald if you need to relay anything to me."

Finding the switch on the comm device in my ear, I changed it to channel three and waited a few seconds for the connection to the satellite. "Chyrel, can you hear me?"

"Five by five," she replied back. "Good to hear your voice again, stranger."

I hadn't talked to Chyrel since Tank's funeral. I'd figured she needed some time.

"Glad to be heard," I said.

"I have Deuce's group on this channel, too. But until they leave the plane, we won't be able to hear them."

"What was he doing down in Nicaragua?" I asked, just curious.

"He said they were on a joint training exercise with U.S. and coalition forces on the ground," she replied. "It turned out that a few people we knew were a part of it, and Deuce offered to fly them home tonight, instead of waiting for the cargo plane in the morning."

"Last jumper away," I heard Deuce shout, wind buffeting his mic.

It takes two minutes to reach 5,000 feet when freefalling from 35,000. They'd have to open by at least 2,500 feet. The seconds ticked by like hours as I waited with Gerald and Ignacio, all three of us looking up at the sky. I heard nothing but the roaring sound of wind over the com.

Trying to talk while face down at 170 miles per hour was an exercise in futility. If you didn't keep your lips held firmly together, the wind would open your mouth and puff your cheeks out like a squirrel hoarding pillow stuffing it'd stolen from an outdoor chair to build a nest for the coming winter.

I waited, holding my breath.

Finally, I heard the first pop over the comm—a parachute rig opening. It was followed by a fluttering noise and less wind. There were five more at one second intervals just after the first. If they'd jumped at one-second intervals, they would have fallen with a good 250 feet of vertical separation. and popping chutes at the same interval, with the last man out opening his first, would roughly double that spacing between each parachute. Then they could fly in a stacked formation toward the south end of the village. The Icarus rigs they were using were far more maneuverable than a round canopy. They could glide and turn, even go up instead of down with a good thermal.

I still couldn't see anything.

Then I heard Deuce say, "Stack up over the south end of the DZ, then spiral down in order."

A few more seconds passed.

"There!" Gerald said, pointing toward the south end of the clearing.

The wide, thin wing of a parachute far above us moved through the light from the five fires, disappearing in the gloom. Another appeared and disappeared, like wispy gray apparitions.

Ignacio stared up in complete awe.

Suddenly, a wing canopy flew out from above the trees at the southeast corner of the village, banking left.

The jumper sawed his hands in opposite directions, steering the canopy back to the right, then flaring to slow forward speed.

ALL AHEAD FULL

The fires illuminated the canopy from below, making the gray tactical parachute look like a giant bird of prey swooping in for the kill.

It flared again, and the jumper landed softly in the sand, pulling the lines on one side to collapse the canopy away from the swift-moving water.

In seconds, the others flew down, each following the same course as the first. The fifth man crashed through the high, delicate leaves of a tree.

"Hoo-ha!" a voice, pumped with adrenaline, yelled into the dark, quiet night, his voice echoing.

All six men landed safely within an area you could draw a fifty-foot circle around. They quickly collected their chutes, draping them over their shoulders as they started coming toward the fire, laughing, and talking quietly.

Ignacio stood in astonishment as they approached in a loose unit. Several villagers came out to see what the fires and shouting were about.

Deuce led the group, and as they drew closer, I easily recognized Tony Jacobs and Andrew Bourke following him.

"Good to see you again, Jesse," Deuce said, extending an M40 rifle to me in lieu of a handshake. "But I shouldn't have to fly a thousand miles and jump out of a perfectly comfortable business jet to do it."

"Good to see you, too," I replied, slinging the rifle on my shoulder, then turning to Tony. "How are ya, Tony? Who do you have with you? Anyone I know?"

"That's a lot of questions," Tony said, his bright smile accentuating the ebony color of his skin.

I nodded at Andrew as he approached out of the darkness.

He smiled beneath his thick mustache, a trademark for Coast Guard chief petty officers. "You remember these guys, don't you, Jesse?"

The next two men stepped into the circle of light the fire created, and I was shocked to see two of Deuce's former DHS operatives.

"How's it hangin', Gunny?" Scott Grayson asked, a sideways grin on his face.

Beside him was another former Marine Recon diver, a burly black man with impressive forearms named Jeremiah Simpson, who we'd called Germ.

"Scott? Germ!" I shouted, waking the other half of the village. "You're about the last people I expected to see."

"Well, I reckon they were still a might ahead of me, mate," the last man said as he approached. He was limping slightly.

"Donnie Hinkle?" I said in disbelief. "Where the hell did you guys come from?"

"I can't say for sure about these other blokes," Donnie said with a grin, "but I hail from Adelaide, South Australia."

I shook everyone's hand, introducing the newcomers to Ignacio and my crew as they came running up from the fires.

"There'll be a test on names later, mate," Donnie said, shaking Gerald's hand. "All ya gotta remember is Donnie's the good-lookin' one."

Gerald laughed as the villagers slowly came closer. I didn't imagine any of them had ever seen a parachute before. And having six men drop in from the sky was, for many, beyond comprehension.

And they were all *heavily* armed.

Ignacio told the villagers that we were there to help; that the farm and lab had been burned.

ALL AHEAD FULL

There were a lot of murmurs from the people gathered around us as the firelight flickered across their faces. I spotted the man who'd let me borrow his rifle and walked toward him.

"*Gracias, amigo,*" I said, extending the Lee-Metford toward him.

He took it and checked the magazine. "*Dos tiros?*"

I nodded solemnly. "*Dos muertes.* One shot, one kill."

CHAPTER TWENTY-EIGHT

By the time Geber got the news about the raid on the farm above the Tawahka village, it was two o'clock in the morning. Then it had taken the man some time to get it all out, since he'd run all the way.

Geber went behind the bar and poured him a mug of beer from the single tap. "Here you are, Mateo. Sit down and rest. I must go outside to make a call."

Once Geber stepped out from under the front porch roof, he was able to connect to a satellite and called Kennar. The man was grumpy but quickly became alert when Geber told him what had happened.

"They will *pay* for this," Kennar spat vehemently. "I will bring some men. How many did you say there were?"

"Seven altogether," Geber said. "Two looked *indígena*. I think they were guides. Mateo said one of those led Carlos, Demian, and a third man, who was wearing a hat and long coat, up to the farm. The others followed. They were four white men and one black man. He said they all looked dangerous and sounded like *Americanos*."

"El Astilla," Kennar breathed. "Señora Castillo-Cortez sent him up there to get rid of the *hombre gato*. He wears a low hat and long coat."

"Mateo said only the *Americanos* and one of the guides returned. He overheard one of them boasting to Ignacio about killing our *soldados*."

"And they intend to stay and process the coca?" Kennar asked in disbelief. "Then steal the product right from under our noses?"

"*Si*," Geber replied, looking up the road in the direction of the village. "I think it will be about two thousand kilos. It will take them days. And there are only six men, but they may have some of the villagers on their side."

"If they returned to the village," Kennar said thoughtfully, "then you are probably right. They will undoubtedly need help but won't start until morning. They could have it wiped out in a day."

"Mateo said they showed no sign of going to sleep any time soon," Geber said, relishing being the one to bring this news to his boss, and possibly being a part of the reprisal.

"How many men do you have?" Kennar asked.

"Five of my top *soldados* will be here in less than an hour."

"I will be there in two hours," Kennar said. "With every man we have here in Cholóma . It will be a blood bath. The thieves and the entire village must pay. We will kill every last person there."

Geber's blood lust raced at the idea of a massacre. "Kill the villagers?"

"Their leader is helping these intruders."

"I will have my men ready," Geber promised.

He ended the call, then made another. "Diego, are you sober?"

"Why are you calling me in the middle of the night to ask if I am sober?" the man on the other end of the call grumbled.

"Get the others together," Geber said. "Meet me at the cantina right away. Kennar is coming and bringing an army."

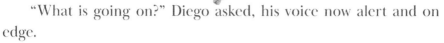

"What is going on?" Diego asked, his voice now alert and on edge.

"*Americanos* came and took our farm," Geber said. "The new one up in the hills. The plants are maturing, and processing began just last week."

"How many?" Diego asked.

"Seven, but they seemed to have lost one in taking the farm."

"So, why an army?"

"Kennar wants to send a message," Geber said, his hard lips pulling back to expose missing teeth. "He has ordered the whole village wiped out."

"The whole village?"

"*Si*," Geber replied. "All of them."

Like him, Diego was also a killer who reveled in hacking his victims to death with a heavy-bladed machete.

"I will contact the others and we will be there within the hour."

"Good. Hurry."

"One thing," Diego said. "Can we take one or two of the young ones? Just to play with for a little while before slitting their monkey throats?"

Two hours before sunrise, Geber heard the sound of approaching trucks. They were coming up the rough mountain road and splashing through the stream.

He led his men out onto the front porch, as, one by one, the big off-road machines pulled into the yard. There were three of them, each one loaded with armed men. Kennar's black Land Cruiser led the way.

Kennar got out quickly and moved to the steps. "Is it secure here?"

Geber looked at him, puzzled. "*Sí*, it is just us."

Kennar hurried to the vehicle's back door and opened it. A figure got out. The jeans and long-sleeved work shirt did little to hide the fact that she was a woman. The gun belt she had strapped around her narrow waist left no doubt that she meant business.

Geber rushed down the steps. "Señora Castillo-Cortez. I wasn't aware you would be coming as well."

"I want the village leader!" she said angrily. "And I want the leader of the men who killed El Astilla! I will cut off their heads myself and you, Geber, you may use their empty skulls as light fixtures right here on this porch."

Geber had never seen the cartel boss so angry. He did, of course, know about those who'd crossed her in the past. That they were all dead and she was still alive was testament to her lethality. He'd also heard the stories of the depravities she'd personally visited on her enemies' leaders.

"Get your men in the trucks," Kennar ordered. "We will hit them at the first light of dawn."

Everyone piled into the trucks, more than twenty men in all, armed with an assortment of handguns, assault rifles, hunting rifles, and machetes.

Five minutes after arriving, the trucks started up the steep, muddy road, headed toward the Tawahka village.

Geber rode in the front passenger seat of Kennar's Toyota, with Paloma Castillo-Cortez in back.

"The Río Plátano will run red for days!" she announced defiantly, beating on the back of Geber's seat.

CHAPTER TWENTY-NINE

When we were in the village earlier, I remembered looking up the river's course. It ran fairly straight for a good way, to a small waterfall that spilled out of a fissure. Rugged mountains crouched around and rose above it.

The waterfall gave me an idea for a diversion, a way of focusing the enemy's attention away from the real danger.

The road ended at the river, where a rope bridge was strung. It was high enough that flood waters wouldn't reach it, and when the river was full, the bridge would be the only way to get from one side of the village to the other. Currently, though, the water level was so low you could cross without getting your feet wet, just by jumping from one dry rock to another. The cartel truck the three men had arrived in was still parked at the foot of the bridge.

After sending Jorge up to where we'd left his truck behind the deadfall, I had him drive it down and park it at a right angle to the road, just inside the clearing. I had everyone switch to the same channel. Then I explained to Jorge and the others what I wanted him to do.

When I finished, he grinned and nodded. "I think it will work."

After grabbing a full gas can that was in the truck bed, he and Ignacio led the hundreds of villagers up into the canyon. They would play a very large part in what was to come.

We extinguished all the fires except the central cook fire, which we let burn down. There was only one way in and one way out for a vehicle.

I sent Tony up to hunker down by Jorge's truck, and when the players were in their positions, he'd block the road with it.

The best ambushes are well choreographed and depended a lot on the natural reaction of the adversary. Knowing how an enemy would react to a given situation allowed a good strategist to use that reaction against them.

I was relying heavily on two things, the first being the cartel's reaction to learning that their farm had been taken over by outsiders, and their cocaine stolen.

I knew their first reaction would be red-hot anger. I'd read many accounts of how these cartels dealt with their enemies and knew they'd be out for blood.

The second thing I was counting on was that they had to know our numbers and makeup. We were outsiders and they'd respond with enough men and firepower to wipe us out. They thought we were six hard men and that'd mean they'd bring as many soldiers as they could.

Since then, we'd doubled our numbers and more than tripled our firepower, including some very accurate weapons in the hands of people who knew how to use them.

Scott carried a crew-served M240 machine gun. Germ would help keep the belt-fed weapon eating, and he also carried an M4 infantry assault rifle. They each had Kimber .45 caliber Desert Warrior sidearms, though I didn't think they'd come into play.

ALL AHEAD FULL

I sent those two men downstream, away from the north end of the village, where the cartel would likely arrive. There were two large boulders leaning on each other, and the gap at the bottom was the perfect place for a machine gun.

Tony and Andrew carried M16A4 rifles and Beretta M9 pistols. The venerable old M16s were highly accurate up to five hundred yards. I sent Andrew across the river to a high ledge overlooking where the cartel truck was parked. Tony would stay with Jorge's truck, both men no more than two hundred yards from where I figured any attackers would park near their other truck. An easy shot for the M16 and on the edge of the AK47's effective range, if that was what they'd be carrying.

That was what the guards at the farm had been carrying.

Axel, Ross, Duster, and Gerald carried only handguns, virtually useless at long range. They all chose spots among the rocks, close to the cartel truck, and were careful not to be in the line of fire from the machine gun and rifles.

Between those eight men, the cartel would be caught in the open, in a withering cross-fire from three sides.

That left me, Deuce, and Donnie, all carrying M40 sniper rifles.

The three of us fanned out to the south, heading upstream. Donnie crossed over to the east side of the river and Deuce and I continued on the west.

"This should be far enough out," I said. "Fan out and elevate."

Donnie found a large boulder he could get on top of, and Deuce made his hide behind a tall, thick mahogany tree that grew out over a house.

I moved farther upstream, having already picked out my sniper hide—right out in the open—a large boulder with a tree growing out of the top of it, directly in front of the waterfall. I'd seen kids playing on it earlier, so all I had to do was find out how they'd climbed up on top of it. I was farthest away, at about 300 yards, but I wanted the enemy to see and hear me.

I was part of the diversion.

There was little to worry about. I was beyond the effective range of an AK and if they had anything better, they'd need someone behind it who was better than we were. Besides, I only wanted them to get a short look. The tree on top of the rock was my cover.

Before taking command of his SEAL team, Deuce had been a sniper himself. As far as I knew, Donnie was still a SEAL sniper. He'd returned to his team when Deuce's DHS counterterrorist team had been broken up.

There was little doubt in any of our minds that the cartel would come. The question was when and how many? They would be expecting to go up against six tough men, so I hoped they'd bring as many as possible.

At 0300, two hours before sunrise, we were all in position, including the villagers up on top of the waterfall behind me. It'd been three hours since the informant took off running down the road. Ignacio said it would likely take him an hour to get down to the bar on the stream. I figured it'd be two hours to get their people together and drive up from Cholóma , then another hour to get to the village from there. I didn't think anything was going to happen for at least two more hours.

"Tony, you have first watch," I said, settling into a comfortable position. "Everyone else, relax. I doubt they'll arrive before dawn."

"Roger that," Tony said. He'd hidden under a large-leafed bush near our truck, in case the cartel stopped to check it out before entering the village.

"I'll spell your eyes in an hour," Germ announced.

An hour slowly passed. Then two. We were within the time frame for the cartel to get there and everyone knew it. They could come at any moment, but my guess was that they'd wait until just before daylight—always the best time for a surprise attack.

Unless, of course, your enemy was waiting to ambush you.

With the first purple light of dawn, I was able to see the whole village below, the truck at the north end, and everyone's position.

Jorge's voice came over the com. "Ignacio says he hears a truck coming down from above."

"Just one?" I asked, my plan already deflating.

"I hear it now," he replied. "More than one. Perhaps three or four, moving down the hill past where we parked yesterday."

"Everyone get ready," Deuce said. "The signal will be when Jesse fires the first shot."

"And I fully intend to let them shoot at me first," I added.

Armstrong's first rule of engagement was to not fire unless fired upon. I'd already broken that rule up at the farm. But I wanted the cartel bosses to see me and to hear the villagers.

When the first truck, a big 6x6 flatbed similar to Jorge's, came out of the tree line, it stopped.

"Be ready, Tony," Deuce said.

I watched through the scope as a man jumped out of the back of the truck and went toward Jorge's, his AK leveled. He carefully checked the cab and, not seeing anything, returned, and climbed back in. I was glad he didn't feel the hood. Though it had been a while since Jorge had driven the truck down, the hood would likely still be warm.

The flatbed lurched forward, and a shiny black Toyota Land Cruiser came out of the jungle behind it. After that, two 4x4 pickups rolled down into the clearing.

When all four had rounded a bend in the road, Tony moved Jorge's truck into position, blocking their escape, and shielding his movement by the terrain.

The men in the first truck jumped out and quickly set up a loose line facing the village, not knowing there was a machine gun, two M16s, and a bevy of handguns behind them.

"Dump the gas now, Jorge," I said. "But wait a couple of seconds before you light it."

As others got out of the trucks, I stood up beside the tree. Just as the smell of the gas reached my nostrils, I heard the whoosh of ignition.

Five gallons of gasoline, dispersed and floating on the surface of the water, would make a huge fireball. Feeling the heat on my back, I spread my legs and raised the M40 in one hand, stretching both arms wide.

"I am the god of hellfire!" I shouted at the top of my lungs, my words echoing off the rocks.

Behind me, flames were cascading over the fall, and as it splashed into the pool at the base, the gas vaporized and ignited. The villagers began yelling in ominous, eerie tones, shrieking and moaning.

"Frickin' cool," Germ said over the com.

A shot rang out from the crowd of cartel members around the trucks. It ricocheted off a rock downstream from me, and far to the left.

I brought my rifle down and leaned against the tree for support, picking my first target—the man driving the Toyota. It was too nice not to belong to the man in charge.

I fired.

ALL AHEAD FULL

Racking the bolt as the muzzle came back down, I reacquired the target, just as a woman get out of the back seat and turned to face me, surprise on her beautiful face, right in front of the man's chest. This all happened in a fraction of a second, as time seemed to slow.

The 7.62mm round, meant for the man's chest, hit her in the forehead instead, then exited the back of her skull, spraying a pink mist all over the driver, who went down, as well.

Just before her face was obliterated, I recognized the woman as Paloma Castillo-Cortez, the head of the Chelóma cartel.

The whole valley suddenly erupted in gunfire, Scott's machine gun chewing through metal and flesh from behind as the riflemen picked the cartel apart from the sides. The others popped up at random, like so many whack-a-moles, firing several rounds from sidearms, then dropping back behind cover.

Deuce, Donnie, and I had no trouble finding targets. There were at least twenty men. My second shot caught a third man, center mass, as he too got out of the Toyota. His body fell on top of the woman's.

She'd come for a massacre, but not the kind she'd encountered.

The firefight lasted less than two minutes. They had numbers, but little else. The element of surprise was ours. We owned the battlefield, having shooters in strategic places, while the cartel was bunched up. We had superior firepower and far better training.

When there hadn't been a shot fired for ten seconds, I knew it wasn't because the cartel had taken cover to try and wait us out. They had no cover. Or more precisely, what cover they did have was only from attack in a single direction. We'd hit them from all sides in a coordinated attack.

Of the three long guns, Donnie had the high ground.

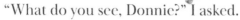

"What do you see, Donnie?" I asked.

"No movement," he replied.

"Anyone close see anything?" Deuce asked.

"They're done," Axel said.

I could see him stand and move to another rock, trying to draw fire, but there wasn't a response.

We waited another few minutes. The villagers came down and began to gather around my rock in small groups. Finally, I climbed down and ordered Tony and Andrew to approach first.

I met up with Deuce and Donnie near the cook fire and we approached from the south, converging around the cartel's trucks, now mostly sitting on flat tires, with glass blown out and raked with bullet holes.

I told Ignacio and Jorge to keep the villagers back until we could make sure all the cartel members were dead. The rest of us advanced toward the spot where the Cholóma cartel had made their last stand. We didn't find anyone alive.

Finally, Jorge and Ignacio came closer, most of the villagers still hanging back.

"What do we do?" Jorge asked.

I turned to Ignacio and in disjointed Spanish asked if he knew somewhere we could dispose of the bodies.

He replied and Gerald translated. "He says there's another waterfall with a high cliff about half a click downstream. The jungle will take care of them."

CHAPTER THIRTY

By the time we'd moved the bodies onto the first of the cartel's trucks—the only one not damaged in the hail of bullets—and then driven the truck down to the cliff, it was mid-morning.

With nineteen bodies on it, the truck was probably overloaded, and the terrain was rough. Moving it through the sand was a chore, but everyone got around it and helped push when it bogged down.

As we grunted and sweated, I thought about what we'd done. We'd killed the cartel thugs up on the mountain without warning. We'd prepared and implemented an ambush against a larger force and succeeded in wiping out what I hoped was the backbone of the cartel.

Was it murder? If arrested and tried, we'd probably all end up in a dark, dingy, Honduran prison for the rest of our lives, which wouldn't be very long.

Paloma Castillo-Cortez wasn't the first woman I'd caused to die. She was an evil woman, and those who'd died with her, both up on the mountain and there in the valley, were equally evil. In my eyes, her sex was irrelevant. She'd murdered men, women, and children as she rose to power in the cartel. The drugs they manufactured and distributed had ruined the lives of untold thousands more. If the justice system in Honduras worked, she'd have gotten the death sentence many times over. She died like those around her—no more than a cockroach under my heel.

I felt little remorse, though taking a human life wasn't done without it. I was dwelling on it more each time it happened.

Her body had been piled into the truck with the others. When we reached the next waterfall, we just let the truck roll off the edge. It exploded when it hit the base of the cliff a hundred feet below.

After that, we said our goodbyes and started the long trip back to *Ambrosia*. It was cramped in the back with the six extra men, but nobody complained. We'd all been awake for most of the night and, despite the bone-jarring ride over the mountains and down to La Ceiba, coupled with the lingering adrenaline rush of the firefight, I'd managed to nod off for an hour.

On the outskirts of the city, Jorge made a stop at a small warehouse.

"There are wooden crates inside," he explained. "All these guns will look suspicious."

We put a large crate into the back, everyone put their weapons in, and we were back on the road in minutes. We were still a sight—eleven men rolling through town in a flatbed.

As we pulled out onto the dock, Savannah appeared at the edge of the rail surrounding the small terrace of our quarters. I waved up at her and she disappeared inside. Then I climbed out of the cab and joined the others, who were unloading the crate.

"Ross, go open the garage," I said.

Matching sets of steps were molded into the yacht's hull on either side. They led from the cockpit down to the swim platform, where the work platform was mounted. Between them, Ross activated the hydraulics and raised the hatch.

As the garage door came up, Savannah descended the starboard steps, walked out onto the work deck and into my arms.

"Are you okay?" she asked.

I arched an eyebrow and got a punch to the shoulder in return.

"I know I shouldn't worry," she said, "Matt told me he'd spoken to you. But I do worry."

"Hi, Savannah," Deuce said from behind her, causing her to wheel around.

"Deuce! Where did you come from?"

He pointed skyward. "Your husband needed a little help."

"Husband?" Donnie asked, grinning, and slapping my back. "You finally found a woman who could put up with you, mate?"

Finn led Alberto down the steps and the dog collapsed on my foot, the thumping of his tail echoing on the aluminum deck.

I scratched his neck while I introduced everyone.

Germ squatted down to eye level with Alberto and grinned. "So, this old jarhead's your pop?"

Alberto nodded.

"Well then, that makes me your uncle." Germ held a massive fist up for Alberto to bump.

Alberto did so and eyed the big man. "My uncle?"

"Why, sure," Germ replied. "Me and him's brothers."

I turned to Deuce. "Will you guys be leaving?"

He shook his head, looking down at the deck, as if disappointed. "You're still not checking your emails regularly. I figured you'd have evolved more with this cushy new job."

"What are you talking about?"

"You have orders to proceed immediately to Bimini."

"And you're coming with us?"

"Jack has a surprise," Deuce replied.

"Then we'd better not keep him waiting," I said, and turned to Gerald. "How much room do you have forward?"

"Five empty bunks," he replied. "Counting the one in the outer armory. Plus a pullout in the colonel's office."

Though Stockwell currently spent most of his time either in Bimini or New York, and Jeff Oswald now used it, the security guys onboard still called it the colonel's office.

"Deuce, you can take the office," I said. "The pullout's comfortable. Get settled and we can get some coffee and food while the crew gets ready to get underway.

"We're all set," Val said, joining us. "Mr. Armstrong sent orders to get underway when you returned. He wants you to call him as soon as you can."

"I'll be on the bridge," I told Deuce, leaving him to make further introductions.

Savannah and Alberto followed me up the steps to the cockpit, then up the outside steps to the next deck and up one more flight to the bridge deck, where our quarters were also located.

"What do you suppose Jack wants?" she asked as we entered the bridge.

"I don't know, but it sounds urgent."

"We'll leave you to it," she said. "Alberto still has his lessons."

"Aww, but Dad just got back, and I want to hear what happened."

"And we both have jobs to do," I said, putting a hand on his shoulder. "Right now, mine is to get the boat underway. And yours is to learn everything there is to know."

There was no way I was going to tell him what we'd done up in the Río Plátano Reserve. At least not until he was older, and maybe not even then.

"And you come get some sleep as soon as we're out of the harbor," Savannah ordered me. "Your eyes look like you've been on a two-day bender with the Port Royal shrimp fleet."

"Aye, Admiral," I replied as Val entered the bridge.

Finn led the way through the inside passageway to our quarters aft the operations center.

"Main engines are online, Captain," Val said. "The deck crew is standing by to cast off."

I yawned and covered my mouth. "Take us out, Val."

She stepped up to the helm and flipped the switch for the ship-wide intercom. "Cast off all lines," she ordered, then went to the starboard hatch to watch the crew, ensuring the ship was free of the dock. "Engage bow and stern thrusters, helm. One quarter power to port."

The helmsman, Kris Carter, toggled two switches. "Quarter power to port, aye."

The ship reacted to the thrusters, moving slowly away from the dock.

"Add the forward thruster," Val said. "Half power for three seconds, then disengage all three."

"Maneuvering forward," Kris said, holding the thrusters as he counted. "One, two, three. Disengaged."

"Starboard engine, ahead slow."

Kris repeated the command and moved the starboard impellor control from neutral to forward. I could hear the mass of swirling water at the stern.

Ambrosia slowly began to creep forward, turning ever so slightly to the left as she did so.

"Port engine, ahead slow," Val ordered, seeing that we were well clear of the dock. "Give me two degrees left rudder."

"Ahead slow," he acknowledged. "Two degrees, left rudder."

Though *Ambrosia* had no rudder, both Kris and Axel still used the term, common among all types of boats and ships. *Ambrosia* used water jets for both propulsion and steering. The two outboard impellors could be rotated up to fifteen degrees and had a cup that dropped down over the outflow to divert water forward and down to make the boat move in reverse. The two inboard water jets were connected to the twin turbine engines and were fixed in place, providing only forward propulsion, and lots of it.

I moved over to the ship's phone and called Jack's office in Bimini.

"How'd it go?" he asked without preamble.

"The Cholóma cartel is done," I replied. "They attacked us in the Tawahka village at sunrise."

"Any of your people injured?"

"No," I replied. "What's going on in Bimini?"

There was a pause before he answered. "You'll have to wait until you get here," he replied. "But make all speed in doing so."

"It's a thousand miles," I said. "At top speed, it'll be tomorrow afternoon before we get there."

"That's perfect," Jack replied. "I'll talk to you then."

There was a click, and the call was disconnected.

I hung up the phone, thinking he hadn't sounded distressed or anxious, and he hadn't used the duress phrase, so I didn't think there was any sort of danger.

"He say what it was about?" Val asked.

"No, but it didn't sound like an emergency. He just wants us there in a hurry."

"In a hurry?"

"Yeah," I replied. "Tell Heitor we'll need the turbines once we're in open water. Set course for the western end of Cuba. The Gulf Stream will give us an added push from there, but we're going to be traveling at fifty knots for better than a day."

The boat moved slowly away from the dock and entered the channel. I remained on the bridge until we cleared the outer markers. Once in open water, I went to the intercom and pushed the ship wide button.

"This is the captain. We're returning to Bimini. Prepare for high speed for the next twenty-four hours."

There really wasn't a lot of preparation to be made. *Ambrosia* rode very comfortably at high speed and if you were inside, you probably wouldn't notice how fast the ship was moving.

The galley was the main thing. They'd have to shut down the equipment and put a lot of stuff away. We'd be eating sandwiches for the next twenty-four hours.

As the outer markers passed astern, Matt came up to relieve Val.

"Don't go anywhere," I told her. "I'm wiped out and in no condition to drive."

"Turbines are online and ready," Val said.

"Do it," I told her with a grin.

Up until now, Val had been, at best, in the second seat during a high- speed run.

"Give me twenty knots on the main engines," Val said to the helmsman.

"Twenty knots, aye," Kris replied, moving the diesel throttles up.

As I watched the knot meter on the chart plotter, the boat began to gather speed,

"Twenty knots," the helmsman said.

"Engage the turbines, Kris," she ordered.

Although the gas turbine engines were only slightly more powerful than the diesels, they operated at a much higher shaft speed. Engaging them at the dock would cause a tidal wave. It was best not to engage them under fifteen knots.

Kris moved the turbine impellor controls into forward and there was a noticeable surge as the two fixed-jet drives engaged.

"Fixed impellors engaged, and systems look nominal," Kris reported.

Val looked over at me expectantly. I quickly checked the radar screen, then nodded at her.

Val turned and looked out over the foredeck at the open Caribbean before us. I knew exactly what she was feeling at that moment.

"All ahead full," she ordered.

Kris's face broke into a grin as he slowly moved all four levers forward, almost to the stops. "Ahead full, aye."

With a combined 21,800 horsepower pushing her, *Ambrosia* continued gathering speed, quickly passing thirty knots, then forty.

Matt moved alongside the helm and checked the instrument clusters and screens for all four engines. "All four engines turning just below the red line," he said.

"Approaching fifty knots," Kris reported.

"Two degrees to starboard," Val ordered, noting a ship on the edge of the radar screen.

She wasn't worried about a collision. Whenever *Ambrosia* was at full speed, we attempted to remain far enough away from other ships to stay off their radar, or at least out of sight, over the horizon. A 199-foot yacht making more than fifty knots raised a lot of eyebrows.

The sea state was a little rough, about two to three feet, with rollers coming at a forty-five-degree angle on the starboard bow. Matt glanced over at me, and I was about to suggest keeping it at fifty when Val ordered Kris to reduce power and hold our speed at fifty knots.

"Fifty knots, aye," he replied.

"Let's change to a four-hour watch, overlapping," I said.

"Oye," Matt replied. "But maybe not for a few hours, yeah? Ya look like shit."

I wasn't offended. I felt like shit.

"You two can stay on top of things?" I asked, checking the overhead clock, and seeing it was already past noon.

"Oye," he replied. "Spell Val here at the first dog watch, then after denner we can start rotatin', yeah?"

The dog watch was an old-school mariner's term. Deck watches were typically four hours, which caused a problem with monotony, as well as feeding the crew. So, the four-hour watch from 1600 to 2000 was broken in two and called the first and last dog watch. By adding a shorter two-hour watch, there were an odd number of watches, ensuring that sailors didn't get stuck on the same watch all the time.

"See you in a few hours," I replied, knowing the ship and crew were in good hands.

"So, what's the big hurry?" Savannah asked, after I'd left the bridge and entered our quarters.

"Jack said to be there by tomorrow evening," I replied. "He wouldn't say why."

"Go get a shower," she said. "Then get to bed. What time will you be going back up to the bridge?"

"Three hours," I replied with a yawn.

CHAPTER THIRTY-ONE

"Jesse," Savannah whispered.

My eyes snapped open, and I sat up on the edge of the bed. That was my normal reaction when awakened. Then the weariness hit me, causing my vision to blur, and I wobbled a little as I stood.

"Here," Savannah said, pressing a warm mug into my hands.

"Mm," I grunted, then took a sip.

It was like spraying ether into the air intake on a cranky diesel on a cold morning. My internal engine fired and coughed. I took another long sip of the bitter nectar of the gods, and my motor started firing on all eight cylinders.

"Thanks," I said, looking at my watch. It was almost 1600.

"You were right," I heard Fernando say from the open doorway where he, Alberto, and Finn looked in at me.

"The coffee turns him human," Alberto said, then he added with finality, "I still think he's a robot."

I made whirring noises as I lowered my other hand, turned stiffly, and did a robot walk toward them.

They both laughed and went back to the table, where Mayra was apparently helping them with math.

I kissed Savannah on the cheek, then went out the hatch and up to the bridge.

"Go grab a bite," I told Val. "And if you don't mind, bring me something back."

"Grady already brought some sandwiches up," Val said.

I glanced at the side table next to the built-in coffee maker, and then went over and took a sandwich at random.

"Then go get some rest," I told her. "Both of you."

"Are ya sure, Cap'n?" Matt asked. "I'm good for a bit longer."

Axel was on the helm and Ross on navigation. Giselle stood beside Axel, observing. She was still learning from Val but was already a very adept yeoman.

"It's going to be a long night," I said. "Get a power nap and come back up in two hours. Val can come up in four, and I'll take a couple of hours off then."

Finishing my sandwich as I watched the horizon ahead, I took an occasional glance at the radar and chart plotter, which although out of radar range, showed numerous ships' AIS locations.

We were already beyond Belize and in Mexico's territorial waters. The sky was clear, and the sea state hadn't changed.

Ambrosia was making fifty knots, and standing on the bridge, my eyes thirty feet above the water, I could see that we were moving but could barely feel it. I was always amazed at how stable the 399-ton vessel was at high speed.

Later, an hour or two before midnight, we'd turn more easterly and cut across about a hundred miles of Cuban territorial waters, which jutted more than two hundred miles into the Gulf of Mexico, between the Yucatan and Florida.

That was the primary reason I sorted our watches the way I did. I wanted to be on the bridge when we did it, though I wasn't overly concerned. The Cuban government and its military largely ignored the wild western tip of the island. We'd be a long way from any Cuban patrol boats, and they couldn't catch us anyway.

I glanced over at Giselle and asked her to go down to the galley and see if her dad and Grady had any fresh fruit.

When she disappeared, I stepped up between Axel and Ross.

"Want to talk about it?" I asked.

"What's that, Captain?" Axel asked.

"About the illegal incursion into a foreign country and the murdering of its citizens."

I knew it probably weighed heavily on their minds, which is why I didn't sugar-coat it, and expressed exactly what we'd done in legal terms.

Ross looked up at me sharply. "No different than shootin' yotes."

"Yotes?"

"Coyotes," he drawled. "When I was a kid, I thought of them as dogs and couldn't understand why my dad hated them so much. Then a pack of them killed my dog, Belle, who'd just had puppies. From that day on, I saw them yotes as nothin' but vermin."

"Those men weren't coyotes," I said.

"Vermin's vermin," Ross replied, checking the radar. "Traffic at ten o'clock. Looks like a pleasure craft."

"Ease it to the right two degrees, Axel."

"Right two degrees, aye."

"What about you?" I asked him, leaning on the console to Axel's left. "Have any misgivings about what happened?"

"None," Axel replied. "They came spoiling for a fight and they got one. But I feel kinda bad about killin' that woman."

"What do you mean?"

"I had a bead on the Toyota's driver, and she stepped into my line of fire."

"I think you missed," I replied. "He was *my* first target, too. But she stood and turned to face me when she got out of the truck."

"You're sure?"

"Positive," I said flatly. "You were at her three o'clock when she looked right into my scope, less than half a second after I'd fired. I saw my round hit her."

Both men looked up at me.

"You okay with that?" Axel asked, a look akin to relief on his face.

"Evil people come in all shapes and sizes," I said. "Men don't have a monopoly on that. She chose her path and walked it. No, I don't have any misgivings about any of what happened up there."

"What about Professor Mejia?" Ross asked.

I peered through the windshield for a moment, wondering what had happened to him. For all I knew, some giant snake in the trees above us could have plucked him from our midst.

"I don't know," I said. "One second he was there and the next he was gone. I think it was intentional on his part. He'd done what he'd set out to do and walked away."

Axel shuddered. "You ask me, that whole thing was spooky as hell."

Ambrosia continued northward. Giselle returned with a bowl of sliced fruit. Small course corrections were made to avoid shipping traffic. Nothing more was said about the ambushes in the Honduran mountains.

When Matt returned an hour before sunset, I stayed on the bridge as a backup set of eyes, but turned over control to him. At our regular cruising speed, one person was enough at night. But at higher speeds, it was always better to have overlapping watches and more eyes. We were traveling the length of a football field about every three seconds. Things could happen fast.

So, the fresh person had control of the ship and the previous remained on duty until the next watch arrived. It meant four hours on duty and only two hours for a nap, but come morning, we could go back to four-hour watches.

"Looks like it'll be a clear night, yeah?" Matt said, as I gazed westward toward a reddening sky.

"Should be," I agreed without looking away. "There's a storm south of Cuba, but it's moving away."

The sun reached the horizon and I glanced at my watch—1710. As a boy, I often imagined I could hear it sizzling when it reached the horizon.

Sunsets where I grew up in Fort Myers, on the gulf coast of Southwest Florida, were almost always spectacular. I guess it was Mam who instilled in me the patience to appreciate the beauty and symmetry of the sun going down. It was a slow process, or it seemed so. When the sun neared the horizon, you could look directly at it, and it was mesmerizing.

The old adage, red sky at night—sailor's delight, was usually accurate. Weather patterns almost always moved west to east, hurricanes in tropical waters being the exception. But in December, there weren't any hurricanes. So, a red sky in the evening usually meant clear skies for the foreseeable future.

Just before the sun disappeared from view, I closed my eyes and silently wished I could be with Savannah forever, as I always did. When I opened them, the sun flashed green for a microsecond, then was gone.

I smiled and raised my mug in salute.

"*Areah!*" Matt exclaimed softly, as he too saw it. "That's the first bleddy time I seen that happen."

"My fifth," I said,

"What's going on?" Axel asked, looking over.

"The Cap'n and I just witnessed a bleddy green flash," Matt replied.

"Kris told me a bunch of 'em saw it two nights ago," Axel said. "From up on the bow. Never seen it myself."

"Probably best to keep *your* eyes on the northern horizon," I said.

"Speakin' of," Ross cut in, "there's a cruise ship out of Cozumel, dead ahead. Heading north just outside Cuban waters."

"Left one degree rudder," Matt said.

Axel turned the wheel slightly and the compass started to come around,

"One degree rudder," Axel said.

"There's another one coming out of Cozumel," Ross said. "Neither is on radar yet, just the AIS."

Cruise ships mostly traveled at night, arriving at their destination ports early in the morning, to maximize the time the tourists on board could go ashore and spend their money.

"How much room do we have between the two?" I asked.

"About fifty nautical miles and closing."

Matt had two obvious options, and I could see the indecision in his expression—slow and wait for the second ship to line up behind the first, as they often did, then go around them on the west side, which would cost us hours, or he could bear east and pass both ships by going into Cuban waters, which could actually save us some time—if we weren't discovered by the Cuban Revolutionary Navy.

I chose a third, slightly more risky option.

"I have the conn, Matt," I said calmly. "All eyes forward. Flank speed, Axel. Rudder amidships. Ross, keep Axel headed to a spot exactly centered between the two ships."

Axel pushed all four throttles to the stops, something we'd done only one other time since I'd taken command. And that had been for only a few minutes.

"Flank speed, aye," Axel said, standing for a better view over the bow.

Full speed isn't the fastest a ship can go. It's the fastest it can go for sustained intervals. Roughly eighty-five percent power. Flank speed is wide open, all engines at the red line. It was for emergencies.

Matt and I moved close to the console. We'd need all eight eyes to avoid anything in the water at nearly sixty knots.

"They'll be barely forty miles apart when we pass between them," Ross said. "Either one could possibly pick us up on radar."

"Beats slowing down," I said. "Or going east into Cuban waters earlier than we need to. They're just leaving port. With luck, the second one won't be paying much attention. And if they are, our radar signature will be small. They might mistake us for a go-fast boat."

Distance was our friend. The range of typical marine radar was fifteen or twenty miles, depending on the ship's antenna height above the water. Modern cruise ships were like floating multi-story hotels with an air draft of two hundred feet or more. A boat beyond that distance would be over the horizon and its radar signature would get smaller the farther over the horizon it was. At twenty-five miles, a powerful radar unit with a sensitive receiver would barely "see" our bridge deck.

Ross called out course corrections as the second cruise ship moved farther out into the Yucatan Channel. We soon passed between the two ships, one nineteen miles to the west and the other twenty-one miles to the east.

Ross watched the chart plotter with the two ships' AIS displays very closely. The radar data was laid over it. Finally, he looked over at me with a grin. "I only picked up a faint return from the one to the west and it was only for a couple of seconds. I didn't receive any incoming radar signal. We're abeam the northernmost ship now."

"Bring us back down to fifty knots, Axel. Matt has the conn."

"Fifty knots, aye," Axel repeated.

"What was our max speed?" I asked Ross, stepping over beside him.

"Sixty-two knots, speed over ground. The current's running north at about one."

"Hull speed of sixty-one?" I commented. "Pretty impressive."

When Val came up to the bridge at 2000, we were still more than an hour from the waypoint where we'd turn toward the Florida Keys and cross into Cuban waters.

Their claim to territorial rights was a geopolitical move that had nothing to do with shipping or commerce. There were no big ports in the western end of the island nation. Mexican and American territorial waters pretty much followed the contours of Florida and the Yucatan, then due west to the border in South Texas. The long, narrow stretch Cuba claimed pointed toward the center of the Gulf of Mexico between U.S. and Mexican waters, extending almost two hundred miles north-northwest from the western tip of Cuba. Its only purpose was to force American-flagged vessels to go around, though Cuba rarely reacted when someone didn't. Otherwise, it pointed toward New Orleans and the U.S. still had a trade embargo with the island nation.

We traversed the short stretch of Cuban water just as Val joined us on the bridge. Matt turned control over to Val, assumed my role as backup, and I left the bridge, telling them to wake me if anything came up.

When I got to our cabin, most of the lights were off. Savannah was in bed reading, a single bedside light on.

"Tired?"

"Exhausted," I replied, taking my shirt off and crawling in beside her with my shorts on.

She turned off the light. "Get some rest. When do you want me to wake you?"

"Two hours," I replied. "Why haven't you asked me about last night?"

"That can wait," she replied. "You need rest if your electronic parts are to function properly, Captain Roboto."

"Thanks," I murmured, kissed her, then drifted off to sleep.

CHAPTER THIRTY-TWO

With the sun past its zenith and heading toward the western horizon, we maneuvered *Ambrosia* toward the dock at Armstrong Shipyard on North Bimini. It had been a grueling run of almost a thousand nautical miles in less than a day.

Several workers waited on the dock to catch our lines. I spotted Jack Armstrong standing alongside the naval architect I'd met on our last visit to the island headquarters.

Just before midnight, we'd entered the Gulf Stream, and rode it all the way around South Florida. It had been a little choppier in Florida Strait than in the Caribbean, which was to be expected, with the east-flowing current doing battle against an easterly wind.

The Gulf Stream was usually avoided for just that reason, except for charter fishing boats going after marlin and sailfish, and those vessels were mostly all in their berths at night. Even the cruise ships tended to stay in the calmer waters closer to the Florida Keys when transiting the Strait, even though going east with the current would be faster.

Matt, Val, and I had rotated two hours in control, two hours on backup, and two hours off all through the night. I finally hit the rack for a solid six hours at sunrise, sleeping until noon.

We'd arrived about an hour earlier than we'd been expected, and though I'd just come on duty, I was feeling it. I'd had almost no sleep two nights before, while we were up in the Honduran mountains, and only short naps the previous night as we raced back to Bimini.

Six hours of deep sleep had usually been enough for me to get back into the groove, but not this time. I knew that when I was tired, I could be irritable and prone to making rash decisions. Recognizing that, I could judge my own reactions, and temper them.

"You still look tired," Savannah said, joining me on the bridge.

"That's because I am," I said, a little too sharply. I smiled at her. "Kick me next time I say I'm going to pull back-to-back all-nighters like that."

"The lines are secure, Captain," Val said from the open hatch on the starboard side.

I pushed the intercom button for the engine room. "Shut 'em down, Heitor. We're home."

"Roger that, Skipper," he replied. "We're scheduled for maintenance in less than a month, so I figure I might steal a couple of mechanics from the yard to help us get it done now."

I looked across the dock to the shipyard area. There was a beehive of activity all around where *Phoenix* sat in drydock. It was my first view of her in person. The only other time I'd seen her, she was just two keel plates and a crossmember.

A crane was lifting a pallet of material from the ground and swinging it over onto the ship's mid-deck, where several men waited. There were dozens more pallets lined up.

"Good luck with that," I said. "The yard looks pretty busy."

"I already spoke to Mr. Armstrong," Heitor said over the com. "He has two mechanics standing by to help."

"Carry on, then," I told him, and turned to Val. "I'm going ashore to see what all the urgency's about. Let the crew know that once the boat's secure, they can go off duty, but stay close. Who knows? Jack might have something too sensitive for the encrypted satellite."

Savannah and I stepped out onto the bridge side deck and started down the steps to the cockpit.

"You know we missed Matt's party last night," she said.

I stopped and turned around. "Oh, crap! I completely forgot,"

"Good thing we didn't," she said, as she stepped past me and continued down to the cockpit.

A motorized ramp was being moved into position, and Peter Jarvis was directing the operator. When he finished, he unfastened the cap rail and folded it back onto the next section.

"We're all set for this evening, Miss Savannah," he said, nodding his head. "The whole crew knows."

"Thanks, Pete," she replied with a smile. "The birthday boy is probably asleep in his cabin."

I followed her down the ramp. "What's going on, and why don't I know about it?"

"We did it on a need-to-know basis," she said, without looking back. "And you and Matt didn't need to know."

"Savannah," Jack said, waiting at the bottom of the ramp, "you're looking as stunning as ever. How do you do it?"

"Thank you, Jack," my wife replied, giving my boss a little hug.

"You remember Will, don't you?"

She shook hands with the architect. "It's good to see you again, Mr. Marshall."

"Please, just call me Will," he said.

"And Jesse?" Jack said, turning toward me. "Well, you don't look so good."

"He hasn't slept much in the last couple of nights," Savannah said. "Is everything ready?"

"Mostly," he replied. "I had everything you requested flown in this morning."

"Are one of you going to tell me what's going on?" I asked.

"I'm sorry," Jack said. "She didn't tell you? When I heard you were planning a celebration for Mr. Brand, and my having you return here wrecked those plans, I contacted Savannah and asked how we could fix things."

"You're throwing Matt a birthday party?"

"He's a bit grown up for that, don't you think?" Jack asked, as we walked toward the office. "We're having a dinner party in his honor this evening."

"A dinner party?" I asked.

"Not just to celebrate his birthday," Jack replied. "While you were running around in the rainforest, he took the exam online and passed it. I just got word this morning—Mr. Brand is now a commercial sea captain of unlimited tonnage, and tonight, I'll be making a special announcement concerning his future."

"What was it you had flown in?" I asked, as Will opened and held the door for us.

"Everything Mr. Santiago and Mr. Lawson asked for so they could make an authentic Cornish fish stew."

"So, what's the big surprise you had us race back here for?" I asked, once we were in the business office.

"There is one other thing of note," Jack said.

"What's that?"

"The power plants arrived yesterday morning," Will replied excitedly. "They're being installed, and everything connected as we speak. The reactors will both go online later this evening, and our first lab scientist will be arriving shortly to start setting up the bio lab."

"I didn't realize *Phoenix* was that far along."

"Oh, there's still eight months of work," Jack said. "But with the reactors online and the ship powered up, things will progress a lot faster."

"You said reactors—plural. *Phoenix* will only have one."

"That's right," Will replied. "The second molten salt reactor will supply a land-based turbine to power the shipyard. Would you like to see them?"

"Do we need a hazmat suit?" I asked, as the door opened.

Matt and Val stepped in.

"*Ambrosia* is secure, Captain," Val reported.

Matt looked around at the four of us. "Wasson?"

"Thanks for coming so quickly, Val," Jack said and nodded at Matt. "We were about to go out and see the reactors. I thought you two might like to join us." Then he turned to me. "No hazmat suits. The system is fully self-contained and automated. One might say it's plug and play. Perfectly safe."

Jack led us toward *Phoenix* but stopped next to a smooth-walled yellow container about thirty feet long. Several men were working at one end, welding large pipes that came out of the wall of the container.

"There will, of course, be a security dome built over it once everything is hooked up. But this reactor will soon power the entire shipyard."

"This is a nuclear reactor?" Matt asked. "A bit small, innit?"

231

"It's a miniature molten salt reactor," Will explained. "Nothing like those that power large cities."

"Another one, identical to this, has been installed in *Phoenix*," Jack said. "Each is capable of powering thirty thousand average homes."

"Or propel a thirty-five-hundred-ton ship at fifty knots," Will added.

"Come take a look," Jack said, leading us toward the ship.

When we reached the drydock, I stood beside the boarding ramp and looked up and down the length of her. At a hundred meters long and ten wide, *Phoenix* was more than one and a half times as big as *Ambrosia*, with three more decks. Easily four times the deck area.

The unpainted aluminum gleamed in the midday sun. But it didn't look like it was going to be like that for long. Workers down at the bottom were readying sand blasters and spray guns to begin the primer and bottom paint.

"Impressive, isn't she?" Jack said, standing next to me.

I turned to face him as most of the others crossed over the ramp. Savannah stayed back.

"Even if she were conventionally powered," I said, "that would be an understatement."

"You're going on salary, Jesse."

I started to protest but he raised his hand and shook his head. "I know what you're going to say. But there's no way around it. We're breaking new ground here, sailing into uncharted waters. You will be *required* to be paid and at a rate commensurate with the position of a sea captain on a nuclear-powered vessel."

"How much?" Savannah asked.

"One million a year," Jack said. "And it's non-negotiable."

"Does it matter what we do with it?" she asked.

We both looked at her, puzzled.

"Um, no," Jack replied.

"Then set up automatic payments to the Rainforest Action Network in the amount of $83,333.33 per month."

I smiled at her. "Your math's improving." Then I turned back to Jack. "Make that seventy grand even and put the rest into a retirement fund for the crew of *Phoenix*."

She smiled back at me. "I'll get busy setting up the details for the retirement account."

"Then we have a deal?" Jack asked, extending his hand.

I took his hand and shook. "We have a deal."

I turned and started over the short ramp, Savannah right behind me. When I put my hand on the ship's rail, I paused. I was getting the same feeling I'd had when I'd touched the first hull plate and we'd set the coins. In the shadow of the superstructure, the aluminum felt cool to my fingers at first, then I felt something like a small spark of static electricity under my hand, as if the metal warmed to my touch. It felt like it could ignite any minute.

"Ah, Dr. Mejia," Jack said from behind me. "You're early."

I spun around and couldn't believe my eyes. Aldrick Mejia, dressed in a white short-sleeved shirt and black bowtie, looking more like a professor than when I'd last seen him, was walking toward Jack, a suitcase in each hand.

"I just arrived by seaplane," Aldrick said, as I quickly retraced my steps.

"How...?" I started to say.

"The principle is called aerodynamic lift, Captain McDermitt," Aldrick said with a smile. "I'm a biologist and a man of science, and though I understand the physics, at times I think it's...*magic*."

I turned to face Jack. "The professor was with us two days ago, when we were at the cocaine lab up in the mountains."

"Is that right?" Jack said with a knowing smile. "Dr. Mejia has been kind enough to offer his services in setting up the bio lab aboard *Phoenix*. Then he will stay on as lead biologist."

EPILOGUE

That evening, the whole crew of *Ambrosia*, Deuce and his guys from Nicaragua, and an equal number of senior technicians, supervisors, and businessmen gathered under a giant tent, the sides rolled down against the cool night air. The temperature outside was relatively chilly, in the low sixties, but a comfortable seventy or so inside. Just the morning before, we'd been in the balmy heart of the tropics.

Savannah, Alberto, and I sat at the head table with Jack, along with Will Marshall, Matt, and Val. Deuce and his team were seated at the next table.

Matt was totally surprised when the main course was served and explained how the simple stew had been the mainstay of Cornish diets for centuries. The dinner had been prepared by a team of cooks, with Marco and Grady overseeing every step.

After a dessert of Caribbean spiced rum cake, Jack stood and was handed a microphone. "Can I have everyone's attention please," he began. His amplified voice resonated from two speakers, but only slightly above conversational tone.

The tent quickly quieted.

"I just want to thank you all for being here this evening," he said, then looked over at me. "I know for most of you the trip was a long and arduous one." He paused as his eyes scanned the room. "I have a few announcements to make."

"Happy birthday, Matt!" a woman's voice shouted from the rear. I glanced over. It was Emma Hall, who worked in the galley.

"Yes," Jack said, motioning Matt to join him. "A belated happy birthday to our guest of honor, Captain Maddern "Matt" Brand."

There was a smattering of applause as everyone looked around at one another, puzzled.

Matt stood beside Jack, and one of the workers handed him a wooden plaque. "Yes, I said captain," Jack continued, handing the wood and brass plaque to Matt. "Congratulations on passing the exam."

Matt took it and thanked Jack, then started moving back to his seat next to Val.

"Not so fast, Captain," Jack said, stopping him with a hand on his arm. "As you all know, the ship being built just over there in drydock will be launched in the coming year and Captain McDermitt has agreed to command it. That leaves *Ambrosia* without a skipper. I'd like to offer you that position, Captain Brand."

"Me?" Matt asked, surprised. "Bleddy hell, Mr. Armstrong, you could have your pick of a dozen fine cap'ns with more experience, yeah?"

"I could," Jack agreed. "But I don't think I could find another man who has as much of the sea in his blood, Matt. You know *Ambrosia* and she knows you. Will you accept the position? Of course, you won't start until *Phoenix* is launched and Jesse moves aboard."

Matt glanced over at Val, who was smiling brightly. "Oye, Mr. Armstrong. I'd be proper proud to sail under your flag."

"And First Mate McLarin?" Jack said, turning to Val. "Would you please come join us."

Val rose, blushing a little, and went to stand beside Matt. The same worker as before handed Jack another plaque, which he passed on to Val.

Jack noticed Matt's puzzled expression. He lowered the mic and said, "She took the exam last month."

"And you knew all along?" Matt asked.

She smiled at him. "I didn't want to say anything in case...you know."

He smiled back. "In case I shagged the dog, yeah?"

She covered her mouth and laughed. "Screwed the pooch, ya emmit."

Jack cleared his throat and raised the microphone. "Congratulations on passing the first mate exam, Val," he said. "I'd like to offer you Matt's position, when he steps up to command *Ambrosia*."

She nodded vigorously and took Matt's arm in her hands, obviously thrilled. "Thank you, Mr. Armstrong. I'd be happy to."

"Thank you both," Jack said, waving a hand for them to return to their seats. "Mr. Livingston, I presume?" Jack said, turning to Deuce. "Sorry, I couldn't help myself."

Deuce, Tony, Andrew, Germ, Scott, and Donnie all rose and walked toward Jack.

Donnie leaned in close by my ear, his hands on my shoulders, giving them a friendly squeeze. "Thought you'd seen the last of old Donnie, eh mate?" Then he joined the others.

"Captain McDermitt," Jack said. "With your approval, please meet the heads of *Phoenix's* new security team. There will be a dozen others, but these men, if you will have them, will be the backbone of your onboard security force."

I was surprised and anxious at the same time. The six men who'd parachuted into the jungle to help us out were some of the toughest snake-eaters I'd ever known.

"Close your mouth and nod, Jesse," Deuce said.

"You'll all be joining us?" I asked.

"Julie and the kids, too," Deuce replied.

"I have one more announcement to make," Jack said.

Suddenly, the lights went out and all the sounds coming up from the crews still working in the dry dock stopped. My chair scraped the concrete deck as I stood, reaching for a gun that I knew wasn't there.

"Please be calm," Jack said in the darkness, his voice still amplified through the speakers. "The PA is battery-operated, since I knew this was going to happen. This will only take a few seconds as the main breakers are rerouted."

The lights came back on. I was the only one who'd been seated when the lights went off who was now standing. And unlike Jack and the others up front, I had my shirt pulled up on one side and my right hand on my belt.

"At ease, Captain," Jack said with a chuckle.

There was nervous laughter as I sat back down beside Savannah.

"It was only the technicians switching power to the reactors. The yard and *Phoenix* are both now running on clean, renewable, nuclear energy."

One entire side of the tent was raised, and all heads turned toward *Phoenix*. She was lit up from stem to stern, inside and out, practically glowing in the darkness. Lights spilled from every hatch and porthole and where there weren't lights, the bare aluminum hull and superstructure sparkled with reflected light from dozens of powerful flood lights all around it.

"*Phoenix* has risen!" Jack shouted.

THE END

AFTERWORD

It was a lot of fun writing this book. I got to dig into a lot of interesting facts about a place I've never been before. I once visited the Bay Islands, many years ago, but never mainland Honduras. I was told by a local divemaster that the coast was similar to the islands, and inland it was about the same, but only for a short distance. Once you started into the rainforest, and ascended into the high mountains, it was like being in another world, different from any other place else on Earth.

I also did a lot of research on the indigenous people of this area. I found it utterly amazing that there are still whole groups of people that have never been contacted by the outside world. As recently as 2014, first contact was made with a primitive tribe in South America. There are many hundreds of other tribes and family troupes whose only contact with modern or even remote society is seeing a plane overhead, or a plowed field from across a river.

And of course, I learned what difficulties were going on in the vastness of South and Central America's interior. Not just the wiping out of the rainforests, which continues at an alarming rate, but also the exploitation of those who call it their home—from the jaguar to the caiman to the indigenous humans.

A special thanks to Dr. Nancy Polstein, PsyD, for her discussion on the difference between nature and nurture, and for opening the possibility in my mind that a child, born in a primitive tribe and growing up in the rainforest, could one day become a professor at an Ivy League school.

Today is Halloween and I'm writing this five weeks before the release of this book. By the time you read these words, *Lost Charity* will have been out for a week. I hope you've had a chance to read it, because Charity can show you a side to some of the characters aboard *Ambrosia* better than Jesse.

Once I finish this afterword, I'll have my fantastic editor, Marsha Zinberg, look it over, while I jump in to see her changes and advice about the story during a week-long rewrite. We've been working together for a few years now, and Marsha doesn't just correct errors, she points out to me why they are wrong.

I look for these types of people everywhere, the ones who not only do their job, but do it with the heart of a teacher.

After editing and rewriting, this manuscript will go to Donna Rich, who has had the final critical eye on my words since the first book. By the time it gets to her, the manuscript is pretty clean, but I wouldn't think of sending anything in for publishing or audiobook recording until she's proofread it for me.

Once Donna finishes, the completed manuscript goes to my friend and narrator, Nick Sullivan. Nick has narrated all of my books and we talk about each character, not just before he starts recording, but often before I start writing. In audiobooks, there's a lot more to developing a character than just telling the reader their height, weight, and hair and eye color. We dig into the characters' backgrounds, where they grew up, what their motivations are. All of this comes out when they speak. Nick handles my many different characters quite masterfully.

But before any of those people see my story, a small circle of friends go over all the technical aspects and sub-plot ideas with me. These are the first to read the story, usually starting within minutes of when I type The End. These men and women come from all walks of life and have such varied and eclectic backgrounds, I'd be forever citing all their expertise, experiences, and accomplishments. They are the unsung heroes behind my books. Many thanks to Jason Hebert, Katy McKnight, Kim DeWitt, Glenn Hibbert, Dana Vihlen, John Trainer, Charles Höfbauer, Alan Fader, and Drew Mutch.

This is the thirtieth book I've written or co-authored. Thirty-one if you count the last few chapters of Ed Robinson's *Cayo Costa Breeze* last year, but that wasn't so much me writing as it was me being the instrument through which Ed and Breeze finished Ed's story.

I still can't believe all this has all come true for me. I've wanted to be an author since I was little. Well, that or a Marine. Or a truck driver. Or an astronaut. But I digress. To those of you who have read the whole, very long, overarching story about Jesse and are reading this latest addition now, I offer my deepest thanks. You have made my dream come true, and I've been paying that forward ever since.

It's been over eight years since I started on this journey, and let me tell you, this vessel would never have left the dock at all without the faith and support of the woman I love. Greta and I were together thirteen years before I wrote *Fallen Palm*. When we married, she taught a daycare toddler class and I worked in a car wash. We've had our ups and downs like any other couple, but the good times have always filled my sails and the bad times faded to distant storms. Thanks for the ride, babe.

Our youngest daughter, Jordan, does a lot of the technical stuff for me, from producing our monthly livestream, to filling orders through our online store, to fixing my phone when I can't make it do what I want. She started reading my books last winter, in order, and is now awaiting this story, along with you, my readers. She will be joining my group of advisors for the next book, *Man Overboard*. Thanks for all the help, Puter.

Humble thanks to our other kids, Nikki, Laura, and Richard, for all the understanding when I've missed out on things these last few years. I know I can't always be there when you want me, but I'll move mountains if you need me to. That goes for our grandchildren, Kira, Lexi, Jack, and Emily, as well. Thank you for the patience you've shown. Being related to a writer is no easy task.

Lastly, a huge thanks to my team at Down Island Press, Down Island Publishing, and Aurora Publicity. I greatly appreciate your tireless efforts in getting my books to my readers in whatever way they want, through whatever channel they use, and in every corner of the world.

If you'd like to receive my newsletter, please sign up on my website.
WWW.WAYNESTINNETT.COM.
Once a month, I'll bring you insights into my private life and writing habits, with updates on what I'm working on, special deals I hear about, and new books by other authors that I'm reading.

If you'd like to receive my newsletter, please sign up on my website.

WWW.WAYNESTINNETT.COM.

Once a month, I'll bring you insights into my private life and writing habits, with updates on what I'm working on, special deals I hear about, and new books by other authors that I'm reading.

The Jerry Snyder Caribbean Mystery Series

Wayward Sons

The Charity Styles Caribbean Thriller Series

Merciless Charity	Enduring Charity
Ruthless Charity	Vigilant Charity
Reckless Charity	Lost Charity

The Jesse McDermitt Caribbean Adventure Series

Fallen Out	Rising Fury
Fallen Palm	Rising Force
Fallen Hunter	Rising Charity
Fallen Pride	Rising Water
Fallen Mangrove	Rising Spirit
Fallen King	Rising Thunder
Fallen Honor	Rising Warrior
Fallen Tide	Rising Moon
Fallen Angel	Rising Tide
Fallen Hero	Steady As She Goes
Rising Storm	All Ahead Full
	Man Overboard

The Gaspar's Revenge Ship's Store is open.

There, you can purchase all kinds of swag related to my books. You can find it at

WWW.GASPARS-REVENGE.COM

Made in United States
North Haven, CT
27 June 2024

54128720R00143